A Royal Ambition

Iris Gower was born in Swansea where she lived all her life. The mother of four adult children, she wrote over twenty bestselling novels, many of which are based around Swansea and the Gower peninsula, from which she took her pseudonym.

She received an Honorary Fellowship from the University of Wales Swansea in 1999 and was awarded an MA in Creative Writing from the University of Cardiff.

Also by Iris Gower

Sea Witch
House of Shadows
Emerald
Bomber's Moon
Spinner's Wharf
Proud Mary
Fiddler's Ferry
A Royal Ambition
Destiny's Child

Iris Gower

A Royal Ambition

1© CANELO

First published in the United Kingdom in 1999 by Severn House Publishers
Ltd

This edition published in the United Kingdom in 2022 by

Canelo
Unit 9, 5th Floor
Cargo Works, 1–2 Hatfields
London, SE1 9PG
United Kingdom

A CIP catalogue record for this book is available from the British Library.

Print ISBN 978 1 80032 775 7
Ebook ISBN 978 1 78863 961 3

Originally published in 1974 under the title Tudor Tapestry and pseudonym
of Iris Davies by Robert Hale Ltd.

Look for more great books at www.canelo.co

Printed and bound in Great Britain by Clays Ltd, Elcograf S.p.A.

Chapter One

"Catherine, my child, what are you doing closeted in your chamber on a day like this? The Princess of France should be outside in the bright sunshine, proving to the world that the de Valois family are proud and indomitable. Come now, pull yourself together."

Catherine dropped her comb, her hands trembling nervously, as Isabel, the Queen, strode into the room her head flung back, her dark eyes glowing.

"Come along girl, what ails you? Are you sickening for something?" Her voice was high and edged with sarcasm. "For heaven's sake, Catherine, stop howling like a baby. You are sixteen years old, and should have learned composure before now."

She paced around the room like a caged tiger, and even in her misery, Catherine could not help but admire her mother's striking, even flamboyant,

I

good looks. Her very skin seemed to radiate a sort of seductiveness; it was no wonder she never lacked for lovers. She had an aura of strength that Catherine greatly envied. Indeed she was compelled to be strong in order to deal with the King's frequent outbursts of violence, but there were times when a little sensitivity would not come amiss.

Catherine brushed back her dark hair nervously. "It's not every princess who is rejected by Henry the Fifth of England." She pressed her lips together and looked away through the window, the sound of revelry drifting in with the hot sunshine, intensified her depression. "He wouldn't have me, not even with the enormous dowry that was offered as an inducement."

"Don't be foolish, Catherine; the refusal is just a delaying tactic on the part of the English." Isabel caught her daughter's arm. "Either Henry wants further concessions, or he intends to make war on France. Now, don't worry about it any longer. The marriage will take place, I am determined upon it." She drew Catherine towards the door. "We will go along to the tiltyard and watch the handsome young men at their jousting; it's a sight that always puts me in a good humour."

The heat outside was almost tangible, the gaily coloured garments of the courtiers threw back the brightness, and the thudding of the horses hooves echoed through Catherine's aching head like thunder. It seemed incredible to her that no one took the threat of war with the English seriously, even though there was ample proof of their strength in the ravaged towns and villages across the land.

She caught sight of Charles, and he waved excitedly. He looked more like a child at play than the future King of France. As she crossed the soft grass towards him, she was aware of the glances that followed her; the ladies were openly curious about her feelings for the English king. Well, let them look! Most of them were no better than strumpets, anyway, falling into bed with whosoever took their fancy.

"Charles, you look well today."

She took her brother's hand, pitying him the smallness of his stature and the fineness of his bones. He was still only a boy, and might grow into manliness with time.

"I won a joust, Catherine. It's a great pity you were not present to see it." His eyes were more luminous than ever, overlarge for his small face and giving him an almost girlish air. "Our cousin landed hard on the turf, I can tell you!"

Before Catherine could frame a reply, Isabel had come up behind her chuckling spitefully.

"No doubt Jean kindly allowed you to win. He always was a good-hearted boy with such a charming smile."

The ferocity of Catherine's emotions almost overwhelmed her. She felt like turning on her mother and raking her sneering face with her nails, but instead she clenched her fists, almost drawing blood from the soft palms of her hands, and forced herself to smile warmly at Charles.

"Well done, brother. No one throws away a joust for kindness' sake; not even our cousin Jean."

Isabel's eyes narrowed menacingly, the colour rising under the heavy bones of her face, and for a moment it seemed there would be a tirade of abuse showered on Catherine and Charles right there in the tiltyard.

Suddenly Charles pointed across the green to where the courtiers were bowing and dipping.

"Look, there's Father!"

Catherine felt her heart dip in fear, but for once the King seemed to be in full command of his faculties. He was neatly dressed, and his wispy hair had been combed into place. She thought of the times when he roamed at large like a wild beast, his clothes ragged and covered in stale food; and his eyes terrible in their emptiness. Quickly she crossed herself. Perhaps it had pleased God to remove the sickness from the King for good, this time.

"Ah, my children, and my sweet little Isabel. It is good to see you enjoying the sports. Isn't the sun beautiful?"

He bent close to his wife. She held her cheek towards him, barely able to conceal the repugnance she felt. The King didn't seem to notice, his watery eyes were on Catherine. The breath almost left her body. She felt pinned to the grass, by his intense gaze.

"I wish to talk to you, Catherine. Come walk with me."

Her father held out his arm. Catherine stepped out at his side, trying carefully to keep up with his long strides.

"The English King must not take away the throne of France, do you understand, Catherine?"

She struggled desperately to think of a suitable answer, but the King waited for none.

"Henry will marry you. It must be! Even though he procrastinates to give him time to prepare for war, it will come to the same thing in the end. An alliance through marriage. It has always been so."

He looked directly at Catherine, his eyes strangely clear.

"Do not let them put pressure on Charles, he is too weak to withstand it; and France will split even more without some kind of king from their own blood."

"I'll do what I can, Father."

Catherine doubted that even in the event of the marriage taking place, she would have any influence at all over Henry. Hadn't Isabel herself called him "headstrong" and "impulsive"?

She became aware that the King's hand was trembling beneath hers. He stopped walking and stared away over her head, as if seeing things that weren't really there.

"If only my brother, Louis had not been so shamefully killed, he would help me now. You know it was our own cousin who struck him down? I have never recovered from that treachery, but then a king is surrounded by traitors all his life. It is difficult to tell friend from enemy."

He was shaking now as if stricken by the ague and quickly, Catherine led him inside, away from the hot sunshine and the prying eyes that followed him speculatively wherever he went. She knew that wagers were made about the length of the King's life, and a mingling of anger and despair throbbed through her so that she suddenly felt unbearably tired.

"Rest Father," she said, softly relieved when his servants came forward to take charge of him. "I will do my best to look after Charles."

She hurried from the room trying to blot out the picture of her father disintegrating into a mindless idiot. It seemed so cruel after the moments of lucidity he had enjoyed for a short time out in the warmth of the sunshine.

"Catherine!" Suddenly Isabel appeared in the dim corridor like a spectre, her lips pressed coldly together, her dark eyes flashing. "What confidence was the King so anxious to impart to you?"

Catherine was startled and bewildered. "I don't know what you mean, my lady."

Isabel caught her arm. "I intend to know what the King said to you. Come along girl. Speak up, before I slap you hard!"

Catherine wrenched her arm away. "His Majesty made a simple request, and one that I doubt I'll be able to comply with; that I intercede with Henry of England on behalf of my brother Charles."

She was gasping and forcing down the feeling of sickness that possessed her, when suddenly Isabel laughed, the tension gone from her face.

"You and Charles, what a bright pair you both make! Even if Henry does marry you, what makes you think he'd take any notice at all of anything you might say? As for Charles, he is nothing but a bastard foisted on me by some lover. He will never rule France while I live and breathe!"

Suddenly it was cold. Catherine stared at her mother, seeing her clearly for the first time as the real power in the land. No wonder her lovers were so attentive. They held more in their arms than a warm sensual woman. When they bedded Isabel they thrust their way into riches and power beyond their wildest dreams.

As if in some nightmare, Catherine saw Charles step noiselessly out of the shadows, his thin face pale; and in the dimness, his eyes glittered strangely menacing. He stood squarely before Isabel, his young face transformed.

"Be careful, madam. Though I may not be strong, I have friends who are prepared to be strong for me. My following is greater than you imagine." He smiled unpleasantly. "By the way, you were quite right about the incident in the tiltyard just now. I did cheat; just be careful mother that I don't cheat you."

He turned and walked away quietly, almost as if he was suspended from chains, the soles of his feet barely seeming to touch the ground.

Catherine was almost afraid to look at her mother. She had expected Isabel to strike Charles for his impertinence but all the time he was speaking she had stood dumb, with an expression of loathing; and yet almost of fear in her face.

"Go to your room Catherine!" The Queen stood tall once more her presence strong, dominating everyone in sight. She lifted her arms towards the heavens. "Was ever a mother burdened by two such wretches as I have given birth to?"

Catherine made her way into her chamber, her hands trembling, though the sunshine was still hot outside. She sank down on to the bed her head aching as if it would burst.

"Marie," she called, "come and help me out of my dress before I choke."

Her maid hurried to her, an anxious look on her smooth young face. "What's wrong, my lady? Not still worrying over the English pig, are you?" She was deft and gentle in her movements and soon made Catherine comfortable, bathing her face in sweet orange water.

"That's better," Catherine smiled. "What would I do without you Marie?" She lay back against the pillows, relaxing. Her eyelids began to droop. "I'm not worrying about Henry," she said drowsily. "There are enough troubles nearer home to keep me occupied. I don't think you should refer to the King of England as a Pig."

Catherine laughed as Marie, quite unconcerned began to neatly fold away the clothes her mistress had just discarded.

"Ah, there is a seam opening here. I will sew that before it becomes worse, my lady. Perhaps at last you are putting on some flesh to cover your bone."

Although the same age as Catherine, Marie's attitude was protective, almost motherly and Catherine wondered suddenly if there was any truth in the tale that Marie was one of the King's love-children, brought up in the royal household by the good graces of Queen Isabel. If it were so, there must have been some very good reason for the Queen's generosity, a salve to her own guilty conscience perhaps?

Catherine held up her slender fingers and examined them against Marie's large capable hands, laughing softly. No one could mistake the maid for a royal princess, but to Catherine it did not matter a jot. Marie was more dear to her than ever a true sister could have been.

"Here, my lady drink this. It will help you to sleep." Marie held a cup towards her and Catherine took it gratefully. "You just put it all out of your head. Why, Henry of England is ten years your senior: quite an old man! You can do better than that with your looks."

Catherine smiled affectionately. "Twenty-six is not exactly ancient, Marie, and he is a king after all."

"*Pouf!* A king may not be a man when it comes to affairs of the bedchamber Lady Catherine and I have had more than one humble man who has been royal between the sheets."

Catherine waved her hand. "Go away, Marie, and let me rest. And don't think I believe all that rubbish, because I don't! Not for one minute!"

Marie winked saucily. "I know I sometimes exaggerate, but only a little."

Silently she left the room and, smiling, Catherine settled herself down to rest.

The sun paler now, cast dazzling orange lights against her lids, and she turned on her stomach, pressing her face into the soft bolsters. What was the use of worrying about any of it? Her fate would be decided without her knowledge or consent, and as a dutiful daughter she would merely have to comply with her parents' wishes. She yawned widely, feeling her body relax deep into the comfort of the bed.

"Catherine, are you asleep?"

She had been, almost, but the sound of her brother's young, anxious voice brought her sharply awake.

"What is it Charles? Is anything wrong?"

In spite of her drowsiness, Catherine felt a tug of pity for the small, pale-faced boy sitting uncomfortably on the edge of her bed. She held her hand to him, and he took it, his face eager. Tears welled like crystals on his long lashes, and with quivering lips he dashed them away.

"I'm sorry Catherine. I just came to apologise for the way I acted earlier. I seemed to frighten you."

She smiled and put her arm around his thin shoulder. "You did frighten me a little, I must confess. You even managed to put fear into our lady-mother, and that is something to see!"

"Well, I meant to scare her. Why does she hate me so much Catherine? And why does she pretend I am not the King's son? It's that which hurts me most of all."

It was a constant source of embarrassment to Catherine that the Queen should so lower herself to insinuate Charles to be illegitimate. And she felt a thrill of anger to see what a profound effect it was having on her brother.

"I think it is something she does because she is afraid of the power you will one day have," she said slowly. "You are the King's son. See how you look like him, and like me too! If you are not his son, I cannot be his daughter."

Charles leaned against her shoulder. "You are so sensitive of other people's feelings Catherine.

Sometimes I feel I won't live to be Charles the Seventh of France."

He sounded so doleful that Catherine laughed.

"Marie!" she called. "Bring some wine. The dauphin is feeling low, and needs some cheer."

Without question, Marie quickly poured some of the sparkling wine, and with a curtsey handed it to Charles, who stared suspiciously into the cup as though he were being offered poison.

"Go on," Catherine urged. "Marie makes it herself and it is uncommonly good for easing a troubled mind and tired body. See how well I feel now?"

After the first few mouthfuls, Charles needed no further encouragement.

"Give me more," he demanded. "It is as you say, quite good."

The long shadows were spreading across the bedchamber, and Marie quietly tiptoed around the outstretched feet of the dauphin, in order to light the candles. Catherine slept like a child, her lashes dark smudges against her soft cheeks.

"It looks as if it is to be left to me to get young Charles back to his bed."

Marie stood hands on hips smiling wryly down at the young boy. He looked defenceless, almost like a baby, but he hung limp and heavy enough in Marie's arms when she tried to get him to his feet. She was panting and breathless, terrified of discovery by the time she got him to his chamber.

"Michel," she called, softly, "come and get the Dauphin into bed."

A tousle-haired youth appeared in the doorway, his eyes dark with sleep. He stared at Marie in surprise, and then down at the young Charles, still fully clothed in his brightly coloured doublet.

"Not attending young boys now are you?" he said teasingly. "Perhaps that's the reason I haven't been seeing you very much lately?"

Marie glanced at him over the sleeping form of the Dauphin.

"Or could it be that you do not please me so much Michel?" she whispered, smiling at him provocatively.

Michel leaned forward and deliberately pinched one of her full breasts. She turned her back on him, pretending anger.

"See to your duties Michel. This is no place for foolishness."

He came up behind her, and his arms encircled her waist.

"Please Marie, come out into the fields with me. It's dark now, and no one will see us. We will be in a world of our own."

She turned and put her arms around his neck, drawing him close. "Perhaps one day we will marry, do you think so Michel?"

Driven by emotion he would have agreed to anything. He kissed her briefly, and released her.

"Give me just a few minutes, and I will be with you."

He was panting a little, and Marie smiled to see the way he quickly drew off the rest of his master's clothes, carelessly throwing the jewelled shoes to the floor. She went out and stood in the dimness of the corridor and when Michel joined her, they ran hand in hand out into the sweet night air.

Something had woken Catherine from her sleep, and now restless she sat staring out of the window up at the deep blue of the night sky, with its scattering of brilliant stars. The air was still warm and the scent of many flowers below her made it unbearably sweet. She heard a soft laugh and saw the flutter of a dress amongst the trees. She knew at once that it was Marie and her young lover, though it had seemed for a while as if the affair was cooling off.

In a burst of moonlight, she saw them clearly, closely entwined with each other, Marie's head thrown back, her eyes closed in abandonment to pleasure. Then a cloud obscured the moon, and the lovers were alone again: in their private world.

Catherine knew envy then, hard and searing! She dropped to her knees at the side of her bed and crossed herself. Perhaps if she prayed for an alliance with England, Henry would change his mind and come to claim her as his bride, after all. She did not love Henry; how could she?

She had never seen him. But he was reputed to be strong, brave and quite handsome for an Englishman.

In any event, nothing could be worse than the life she lived now, surrounded by spite and plots, her poor father out of his wits most of the time, and her mother lusting after every new young gallant who came to court. Even Marie had someone to love her, while she, Catherine de Valois, princess of France, had to keep herself unspoiled so that her bargaining value would be high enough to attract a king.

"Please heavenly Father, I do not wish to spend my lifetime waiting alone in my room. Send King Henry across from England, and make him want to marry me."

She climbed into bed and snuggled under the covers; though the night was warm she shivered suddenly, and her teeth seemed to chatter, as if she had a fever. She pulled the bolster over her head, trying desperately to shut out the sounds of the night, but most of all to muffle the sound of the occasional soft laugh that came from the corner of the field, just under her window.

Chapter Two

The hot August sun scorched down on the people lining the banks of the harbour.

"Give them Frenchies what for lads!" shouted an old man waving a thin arm towards the embarking soldiers. The water was alive with ships, they rose and fell like so much flotsam waiting for the tide to turn and carry them out to deeper seas.

"Will you just look at those archers." A woman with a bundle of washing under her arm stared in admiration at the bulging muscles of the long-bowmen. "I wish I was going with them, I'd do a good job of serving them, the whole ruddy lot!" She laughed coarsely, and a nobleman watching the proceedings from the comfort of his carriage, poked her good-naturedly with his walking stick.

"I think even you would find that undertaking a bit strenuous! It's said that the King has twenty-four thousand archers, and six thousand men at arms!"

A roar of appreciative laughter swept around the crowd.

At last the tide was right and the graceful ships became alive with purpose, heading out of the calm bay and into the open seas. A great cheer went up from the people on the banks.

"Long live King Henry the Fifth, God save the King!"

On board the royal ship, there was an air of controlled excitement. Orders rang out on the hot summer air, and as the sea birds wheeled overhead many of the men made the sign of the cross, and prayed for a safe journey.

Owen Tudor watched the receding shoreline. Dazzled by the splendour of the spectacle, the bright banners waving in the fresh sea breeze and the glint of sun striking on steel, seemed like a dream to the young Welsh boy. It was a far cry from the austere Welsh hills, and the sternness of his upbringing, though already he missed the warmth of his parents' love and most of all the sweetness of the Lady Elizabeth who was now promised to someone else. He thought of her as he'd seen her last, her black hair blowing fiercely in the strong mountain winds, and her small frame pressed against him wishing him goodbye. And there had been tears in her eyes.

"Your first campaign, sir?"

He turned self-consciously, as if the man at his side might be aware of his thoughts, but there was nothing except politeness on the smooth face that looked at him. It was a good strong face and sunbrowned, though Owen guessed that the man was still below twenty years of age. His arms were well-muscled, giving away his occupation as archer, in the King's guard.

"Is my lack of skill so obvious?" Owen smiled wryly. "Yes, it is my first campaign. I suppose you are well experienced in wars by now. I envy you."

"Don't envy me; your first battle is like your first woman. A thing to be savoured." He held out his hand in friendship. "I am Thomas Cooper from Somerset, one of the King's own bodyguard. Mostly people call me Tom, though."

Owen stared across the blue swell of the sea. "What is France like? Is it true that the men are all weaklings, walking about in fancy clothes?"

Tom snorted with laughter.

"Is that what you've heard? Don't you believe it! They are good hard fighters and brave. Though not as well trained as we are, naturally." His eyes shone. "The women are beautiful little creatures, dark eyed and golden skinned; an appetising change from the rosy pinkness of an English girl. And hot blooded, too; must be the sun that makes them that way."

Owen laughed delightedly. "You make me long for France; I can hardly wait. Stay close to me Thomas Cooper, I've a feeling we will enjoy some adventures together." He sobered suddenly. "I feel in my bones that this will be a triumphant war for us, and that we are fortunate to be with King Henry, in this."

Thomas nodded, sensing some inexplicable power in the young boy, and he shivered suddenly fingering the cross at his throat.

–

The moon was silvering the water when land was sighted and Owen woke effortlessly from sleep, anxious to get his first view of foreign shores; surprised to find that it all looked very ordinary, just like any other bay. The fleet of ships moved like silent shadows, and Owen strained every muscle, trying to penetrate the darkness of the shore with his aching eyes, in case hostile Frenchmen were waiting to attack. Tom appeared suddenly at his side.

"The King is making for Harfleur, on the north bank," he said softly, grinning as Owen looked at him in surprise. "No he hasn't confided in me personally, but I've been this way before, and Harfleur is the chief port – so it's the obvious place to start the attack."

Owen looked at him with respect, for his sound common sense, wondering if he ever felt the chill of fear in his blood.

Tom put his hand reassuringly on Owen's shoulder, as if reading his thoughts. "It is the waiting that cramps the muscles and brings the bile to the throat; once the action begins, your blood will race anew, and you will feel really alive and eager to have the victory. Come we must prepare to step on to the earth of France."

Suddenly the silence of the night was shattered; men were calling to each other, and the archers were already busy with their bows. The siege of Harfleur had begun.

–

The ground was hard, but Owen slept soundly, beside him Tom carefully flexed his bow, examining it for any weakness that might have developed in the wood. He glanced at the sleeping boy, smiling indulgently. Owen had imagined a sharp short battle with immediate triumph, not this drawn-out uncomfortable siege. Already there were signs of maturity in the new angles of the boy's face, and his shoulders had a breadth which had previously been lacking.

Owen Tudor had come to France as a boy, five weeks ago, but he would return to England a man. He had acquitted himself well in battle and deserved the few hours' rest the King had granted him.

The grey light of dawn began to streak the sky, and Tom leaned forward and shook him gently. "Owen, it's morning; time to get started again."

Immediately Owen's eyes were alert. He sat up, holding his fingers to his lips, for silence. "Someone is coming."

Tom could hear nothing, but quickly scooped damp soil over the fire and drew, with Owen, behind the shelter of the thick bushes, which were damp with early morning dew.

A few minutes later, a group of Frenchmen came into the clearing, two of them supporting a third, who had a bright 'kerchief tied around his chest. They sank down to rest, talking rapidly in their strange-sounding tongue, and Tom fingered his bow warily.

Suddenly, Owen gripped Tom's arm. His eyes were bright as he moved carefully away from the Frenchmen.

"We have no quarrel with them now," Owen whispered, "Harfleur has surrendered."

A glow of satisfaction swept through Tom, and suddenly all his weariness was washed away.

"I knew this was going to be a good battle," he said, "and this is only the start. We must go to the King's tent. He'll be needing us for the march into the town."

They moved forward, quickly, watching for stray soldiers, and Tom attempted a warning.

"Owen, remember the men are weary; some of them ill." He paused, struggling for words. "If you see sights that offend you, try to understand the men need release."

But Owen was already hurrying forward to bow before the triumphant monarch.

The streets of Harfleur were in chaos. All the townsfolk seemed to have turned out to sullenly watch the English in their triumph. The King's archers were strategically placed to guard the King, as a precaution against a hidden rebel who might fancy an attack at close quarters.

From his position behind the King, Owen stared curiously into the crowd. Where were the beautiful women Tom had told him about? Most of those he could see were far from attractive, sallow of skin, and enormously fat. They stared in silent hostility at the passing army. The dirty children with their large brilliant eyes were the only ones to show any animation; they pointed at the King, and chanted something in their strange tongue, until hushed by irate mothers.

Then, in an upstairs window, Owen caught sight of a girl about his own age, her dark hair streaming around her face. For a moment their eyes met. He lifted his hand in salute and she immediately slammed the casement shut.

"You won't find them all so retiring, young Tudor," the King said in amusement. "We will have some fine wenches to attend us soon; and most willingly, too!"

For a moment the King of England and his youngest gentleman-at-arms seemed almost friends; and then Henry spurred his horse forward through the streets of the conquered town.

—

The army moved along the coast in the direction of Calais, the numbers drastically reduced, more by the war-sickness than from attack by the French. Owen had never felt better in his life in spite of the fact that he had indulged himself to the point of exhaustion with a sweet little lady by the name of Marguerite. She'd been all that a French lady should be, and most of all, she had been particularly accommodating in her affections.

He caught sight of Tom among the men of the bodyguard and lifted his hand mockingly. No doubt, the archer had made the most of the brief rest before the march to Calais had got under way. Occasionally, a man would drop from the ranks and crouch beside the road clutching his stomach in agony. There was nothing that anyone could do except cross himself and hope the dysentery would pass him by.

The King had hoped to cross the river Somme at Blanchetaque, but to his surprise the ford was heavily guarded, and there was nothing left but to go further up the river. The men were tired, but Henry rode among them urging them forward, and Owen felt tears of pride at the sight of his king's courage and determination. It wasn't until they had almost reached the river's source that the army were able to cross, and all the men moved more eagerly, knowing that once they reached Calais, the next stop was home.

Suddenly there was consternation among the lords surrounding the King. One of the outriders had returned at full speed, his horse sweating and shaking with exhaustion. Owen pressed nearer in an effort to hear what was being said.

"The Duke of Orleans waits with the Constable of France, and a huge army of nobles, Your Majesty," the man gasped. "They have barred the road to Calais. It seems we must fight or surrender."

The King looked thoughtful. "As they outnumber us, we must outmanoeuvre them; and remember gentlemen, the French do not have our military prowess."

Owen gasped in amazement as he caught sight of the French army placed in ranks between two woody glades. They stretched across the road like a black mass, reaching back as far as the eye could see.

"They outnumber us seven to one!" Owen said in disbelief.

The King moved ahead. "Place the stakes!"

His voice rang out, and foot-soldiers hurried to do his bidding, pointing the jagged spikes forward at an angle, making a lethal wall to check the rush of French horsemen. Behind the spikes the archers were in position, and Tom was one of the first to place an arrow in his bow and strain his muscles ready for the command to fire.

At the wall of stakes, the horses faltered and the Frenchmen were compelled to wheel the animals away. The hail of arrows fell with unmerciful precision, and Tom moved smoothly, selecting an arrow, fitting it and loosing it into the mass of men and horses without stopping to think about his actions. Even when his muscles began to scream in agony at the ceaseless movements, he didn't slow his pace.

Too late, he saw the flash of a blade descend towards him; he was blinded with light before he fell unconscious to the ground.

As the day died, so did the battle, and against all odds the English army were the victors. The Duke of Orleans was taken prisoner, and the Constable of France, along with many other French nobles, were lying dead on the field. Owen, now that it was all over, felt tired and dispirited; he prepared as others were doing to roll up in a blanket, and sleep.

He became aware of the throb of the wound on his wrist, and the ache in his head, where a French knight had hit him with bare fists, having lost his weapons. He wondered how Tom was faring. He'd managed to drag him from the field, but the wound in his neck had been deep and vicious, and his face grey beneath the mud of the field.

"Owen! Thank God you are safe."

He looked up in amazement to see Marguerite running towards him, her cloak flying behind her like a scarlet banner. With a cry, she flung herself into his arms.

"I've been searching for you for hours. I was so afraid you had been killed."

She clung to him, tears streaming down her cheeks. Owen kissed her, brushing the hair from her face.

"Come, climb up on my horse; this is no place for a woman."

"So many dead, I can hardly believe it," she said amid tears. "I know I should hate you, Owen Tudor, but I prayed to God to keep you safe."

She was too overcome to say more, and in silence they left the battlefield.

–

Henry was resting, well pleased with himself and his men. Seven thousand of the French lay dead; brave men, but badly led, and not equipped to deal with the military efficiency of the English army.

"The day of Agincourt will long be remembered," he said with satisfaction. "We proved that skill may win over sheer weight of numbers. Send for my bodyguard, gentlemen, I wish to thank them in person for the work they've done this day." When the men were assembled he spoke a word to each of them, stopping before Tom who was heavily bandaged about the head and neck.

"We wish you to be seated." He handed the man his own goblet of wine. "Drink, and may your wounds heal well and strong before we reach our home shores."

"If it hadn't been for young Owen Tudor, I would have been lying dead on the battlefield, Sire," Tom said.

The King raised his eyebrows. "Yes, I saw that Tudor acquitted himself well. I have been thinking about giving that young man a knighthood. Where is he now?"

Tom looked at him almost fearfully. "I heard he left the field with a woman, Sire." Henry threw back his head and roared with laughter. "Rest now, we make for Calais before very many hours have passed."

He sank down on his couch, the exploits of Owen Tudor having excited his imagination. He only wished he had his sweet little English mistress by his side, pink and golden like a summer's day.

—

Marguerite knelt on the edge of the bed, like a cat about to pounce. Owen, in his amusement, was quite ready to be attacked, particularly now that he had washed the smell of battle away.

"Come little Marguerite, why sit looking at me as if you would like to eat me? Why not join me beneath the sheets?"

Silently she slipped her dress from her shoulders. Her waist was small, and her skin brown with a healthy sheen to it. She held him close, kissing his lips, gently.

"I thought you might be too weary to pay me any attention, my lord," she whispered, nibbling his ear. "Does your arm hurt now?"

Owen glanced at his wrist. "No, it doesn't hurt at all. You've done a very good job." He drew her closer. "You are very sweet to me. I am more fortunate than the King himself." He kissed her, drawing the sheets over her slim body. "You know I will move on in a few hours, and there is no question of taking you with me. This will be our goodbye."

She held her hand over his lips, her eyes deep with emotion.

"I don't want to think about the future," she said, as she laid her head against his shoulder. "The King must return, and I pray that you will come, too. There will be a marriage; our Princess Catherine waits for your Henry. They say she cried aloud in her room because he has not taken her for his wife yet."

Owen nodded. "It is true; they must wed some time, and if Catherine is anything like you, I don't know why the King hesitates. What is she like, your princess?"

Marguerite's eyes glowed. "She is young, about your own age, and very pretty; her face is a trifle long perhaps, but she is dainty and so tender-hearted. They say she has to keep the peace between her mother and her brother, Charles, who is even younger, and very spoiled I think. One day you may meet her, and then you will think she is much more beautiful than your little Marguerite, who is growing too old for you already."

She pinched him playfully, and he held her tight against the hard muscles of his chest.

"I can hardly bring myself to leave you," he said softly, "but the King intends to press on before daylight. I'm sorry I've no gifts for you Marguerite. You deserve some token of my regard."

She looked up at him, her eyes shining. "You have given me a token." She placed her hand meaningly over her stomach. "I believe I am going to have your son."

"Marguerite, how will you explain it to your family? You will be disgraced!" He took her hands in his. "As soon as possible, I will send you money, I promise you won't be deserted."

"Don't worry about me, Owen. I have friends who will help me with a plan I've formed to make myself a widow of the battle. How can anyone disprove it with so many dead?" She smiled. "Don't have regrets Owen, I have none. Go now, the King will be displeased if you keep him waiting. God be with you."

When she was alone, Marguerite threw herself on to the bed still warm from his body, and cried as though her heart would break.

–

In the grey light of the morning the weary army pushed on towards Calais. Tom's neck ached and his feet were sore and blistered inside his boots, but worse than all the discomfort was the pain inside him because at each village they passed, there were groups of weeping women and fatherless children.

He caught sight of Owen Tudor riding proudly at the roadside and he envied him for the strong horse beneath him. The boy looked as fresh as if he'd spent the night alone instead of in the bed of some wench. Tom grinned, it must be fine to be endowed with such charm of person that the women just clamoured for your attentions.

The sun was rising as they entered the town of Calais, the people stood and watched in dumb hostility as the army, with banners waving, marched through the streets.

Tom tried not to see the dark angry faces. The air was warmer now, and the pain in his head and neck was worse. He'd give a year's pay for a cool glass of ale, and a green field to lie on. Soon the tangy smell of salt was in the air and then the sea came into sight, dazzling a rich sapphire blue.

It was good to be going home. Owen helped Tom to slip the bow from his shoulder and the grey goose feathers fluttered in the breeze.

"We'll have a hero's welcome all right," Tom said, glancing up at the sky, "but how long will the joy of the people last when they know that many more battles must be fought before England can be sure of keeping the ground already gained?" He glanced at Owen. "Not that I'll fight again; my right arm has lost its power since I received that wound. I never did thank you for getting me out of there."

Owen waved his thanks aside, and went below to see if the King needed anything.

"You have brought me luck, Owen Tudor, and yours must be one of the first faces the crowd will see when we return home."

Owen bowed smiling at the King. "I am honoured Your Majesty."

When he stood again, he realised that now, he was as tall as Henry, if a little thinner.

"Well, young Tudor, it seems we have made a man of you. Or could it be the work of the French maidens, I wonder?" He smiled indulgently. "Remind me to keep my favourite mistresses away from you!"

Chapter Three

The noise and chatter of the ladies tired Catherine. She rose to her feet abruptly, and left them to their interminable stories about various amorous adventures. It set her teeth on edge to listen to them.

She shivered as she entered the coolness of her chamber.

"Marie, are you there? I would like a wrap please." She moved across to the window. "September is fading fast. Soon winter will be here, and I am still not married."

Marie placed a shawl carefully around Catherine's shoulders. "My lady, you should take more care of your health. Henry of England would not want to marry an invalid, would he now?"

Catherine shrugged and leaned over the window ledge.

"It is four years since Agincourt. Henry has conquered much of France, and still he hesitates to make me his bride. That is not very flattering is it?" Suddenly the tears rose and spilled down her cheeks. "How long do I have to suffer this humiliation? Why doesn't my mother try and make some other match for me before I am too old?"

The sound of horses' hooves drew Catherine's attention to the window. To her surprise she saw her brother Charles rein his horse, and offer a mock bow.

"Tears Catherine? Our mother does not deal well with you, I see, but I may have a good husband for you before long."

He was immediately hushed by his friends, and he glanced quickly around, the colour rising in his thin cheeks.

"God go with you Charles," she said softly, leaning as far out of the window as she dared. She saw him grimace.

"I hope He is with me now because I have to see our lady-mother on business!"

He waved and spurred his horse forward and Catherine watched until he was out of sight.

"Here is your drink, my lady." Marie held a cup brimming with a thick golden liquid and tentatively Catherine tasted it.

"It is quite pleasant," she said smiling her thanks. "I hope it is effective too." She drank deeply. "The Dauphin has just arrived to see the Queen. That will put her in a bad humour for days. You know how she hates him." Already she felt her taut muscles begin to relax and swiftly she drained the cup. "Had you been born in some other time, you might have been an apothecary, Marie. I think I'd better get into bed."

It was comfortable and warm between the sheets, and Catherine felt a sense of well-being as she lay on the scented cloth that Marie had thoughtfully provided. She wondered idly what plans Charles might be hatching to marry her off. She was tired of being a virgin-princess, and in any case it seemed that life was passing her by.

"Marie," she said sleepily, "what is it like to have the love of a man?"

She lifted herself on to one arm, her dark hair spread about the bolster like shining silk. She saw the uncertainty on Marie's face and read the changing expressions well.

"I don't want a romantic story, I get quite enough of those from my ladies. Tell me the truth."

Marie grinned. "When I loved Michel, my lady, it was sweet and wonderful like true love is supposed to be, but since he's left me, I have found no one to give me the same feeling."

Catherine looked at her steadily. "Then you think there is just one man for one woman?"

Marie frowned in an effort to concentrate. "I don't think that, my lady, but sometimes one love will come along that will outshine all the others. It is difficult to explain."

Catherine smiled, and fell back against the pillows. "Never mind. I'm too tired to think any more. Put the covers over me Marie. I must sleep."

–

Charles moved across the hall as if treading on eggs.

"I have arranged to meet the Duke of Burgundy on the bridge at Montreau. It has become necessary for me to negotiate with him." He was aware that his mother was watching him, a contemptuous smile on her hateful face. "Someone has to make a move, Mother."

Isabel's laugh, thin and hard, echoed along the corridors.

"Charles, if I did not know you better, I would imagine you had come to this decision on your own." For a long moment, she gave her attention to the reflection of herself in the mirror. "As I do know you, I assume you have powerful friends – not that it will do you any good. Burgundy will not raise a finger to help you."

Charles felt the colour rise to his thin cheeks. "I don't see you make any helpful suggestions, Madam, and you are being absurdly short-sighted in this matter. Why not help me? I am your son, am I not?"

Isabel turned on him fiercely. "It is to my shame that I must agree with you. You are my son, unfortunately. Remember, I have repudiated you. I have no time for your foolish ideas. You will never be King of France. Now please leave before I have the guards throw you out."

As Charles stared at her in bitter enmity, the Queen felt a pang of fear. It was true that Charles had a large following in the southern parts of France, though she couldn't understand such loyalty herself. Perhaps it would be wise to speak a little softly, just in case anything came of his wild schemes; after all, she could not always hold men with her looks.

Charles had not seen her uncertainty, just the cold implacability of her face as she stared at him. He quivered with anger. His mother had always made him feel less than a man, and once more her icy contempt had diminished him. He left the palace under a cloud of anger and misery, but she would see, oh yes! something must come of the meeting tonight.

"Let us ride!" he shouted to his men, and galloped his horse as if a thousand devils were after him.

–

Catherine seemed to be swimming through a sea of sticky honey. She wanted to sleep, but voices, loud and insistent, were penetrating her dreams. She sat up with difficulty and saw the moon was silvering her chamber. The voices rose again, almost like a wave, and Catherine forced herself to get out of bed, tottering slightly, still half under the influence of the potion Marie had given her.

Fear began to churn inside her; something must be wrong. She was used to the sounds of laughter and gaiety that swept along the corridors of the palace during the night-time, but this was different. There was the voice of a man, young and obviously hysterical, raised in anger.

Quietly, Catherine made her way along the cold corridors and unnoticed, slipped into the large chamber. It seemed to be crowded with people and the attention was turned upon young Phillip, his face streaked with dirt, and his eyes red-rimmed and weary.

Isabel was at her most regal, standing erect, her hands clasped to the bodice of her red silk gown. She saw Catherine and gestured imperiously for her to come forward.

"Charles has murdered the Duke of Burgundy!"

The words rung around the room and Isabel allowed a glimmer of a smile to linger around her lips for a moment, well pleased with the effect she had created.

Catherine swayed a little. It must still be a dream. Her brother Charles couldn't kill anyone. As if reading her thoughts, Isabel shrugged her white shoulders.

"Oh, I doubt if he had the courage to do the deed himself, but in his name murder was done."

Phillip made a strangled sound of grief and anger, and put his head down on his hands. Isabel spun towards him.

"Phillip, remember, you are Duke of Burgundy now. You must behave with courage."

After a moment he regained his composure and lifted his head, looking around at the assembled company with determination.

"We will make Charles suffer for this, and the first step will be for an alliance between England and France. Catherine must marry Henry, and we will agree to his terms that their heirs shall rule France, but only after the death of our beloved king."

Startled, Catherine looked at her mother, but Isabel had eyes only for Phillip. A look passed between them, and it was clear that he was saying just what the Queen wanted him to say.

"I will not betray my brother in that way!"

"Go back to bed child. These are matters for others to discuss. You will be advised of our decision later." Turning from her, Isabel placed her hand on Phillip's shoulder. "Come, we will discuss this in more comfortable surroundings."

She laughed softly and as the ladies dipped into a curtsey, Catherine heard one of them murmur, "The Queen likes them from the cradle these days, it seems."

Closing her eyes against the shame and pain she was feeling, Catherine somehow found herself back in her chamber; quickly she climbed beneath the covers, shivering in every limb. Her brother Charles had turned murderer, and because of that she would marry the King of England, after all.

–

The June sunshine bathed the city of Troyes in a mellow haze encouraging the thirsty citizens to drink deeply of the sweet wine that was all the better for being handed out free in honour of the marriage of their beloved princess Catherine and Henry King of England. The flow of wine coaxed the people in the street to forget that the same Henry had ridden across France leaving devastation and death behind him.

"God bless Catherine de Valois."

The roar went up among the crowds, and hearing it Catherine shook with nerves. Her gown, encrusted with pearls, was hot and heavy, and her head was beginning to ache with the effort of standing erect. She risked a glance at the man at her side and was not displeased. Henry was every inch a king; a mature and well-formed man. And Catherine knew she was lucky not to be married off to an old and ailing monarch, a fate common to a princess! She would probably cease to be in awe of him once the interminable ceremony was ended, and she was truly his wife.

She caught a glimpse of Isabel and Phillip standing close together, a look of satisfaction on their faces. Once the marriage service was over, Isabel swept forward to embrace the King of England, placing both her hands on his arms and reaching up to kiss him in a far from motherly manner.

"I must be allowed to salute my son," she said smoothly. "Wine, bring wine!"

Catherine was grateful for the respite; soon she would be led with Henry to the royal bedchamber. The prospect frightened her, and she looked shyly down at her hands as she heard one of the courtiers make a far-from-tasteful joke.

Suddenly she became aware of someone bending over her hand. She looked up at a tall handsome man; his hair shone like red gold in the sunlight, his eyes looked directly into hers so that she suddenly felt weak as if a great sea wave had washed over her, turning her like a pebble on the beach.

He murmured some pleasantries, but he had a strange accent, and she didn't know what he was saying; but she was stingingly aware of him as if he had put a spell on her. It was a foolish and dangerous way to feel, particularly now that she was Queen of England.

The ceremony of leading the couple to the bedchamber was soon over, and Catherine stood passive, waiting for her husband the King to make some sign that he cherished her, or at least had some regard for her as a woman. Instead, he drew her rather impatiently towards the large bed and then she felt his weight press against her and she was no longer in possession of herself. She was being invaded, and the physical pain was nothing compared to the pain that had come to rest in her heart.

To Catherine's humiliation, Henry spent only one day with her.

"I have to go on and conquer the rebellious regions of France, you understand Madam; it is for our heirs."

He spoke abruptly as his attendants helped him into his armour, and then he lightly kissed Catherine's cheek signalling that he was ready to leave. With mixed feelings she watched him ride away.

There was a stir in the room behind her, and she turned to face her mother who had swept into the royal chamber unannounced.

"What is wrong Catherine? Why is your husband riding away so soon? He will not beget heirs that way!"

Catherine shook her head, wincing at Isabel's outspoken vulgarity.

"Nothing is wrong; in fact the King is convinced that I must be already with child. He is a man of great vigour."

Isabel scrutinised her face.

"You certainly look exhausted. I trust that you have proved yourself worthy to be called my daughter, though I still think it strange that Henry leaves so soon." She sat herself down on the bed. "In any case, it is no longer any concern of mine, because this must be our goodbye. The King has left instructions that you be removed to Windsor immediately."

Catherine turned away quickly so that her mother would not see the distress her words had caused. Henry had not chosen to give her the information himself, and she hadn't bargained on the move coming so quickly.

"Mother, I would like to take Marie with me," she said at last, and saw immediately the hesitation on her mother's face. It wasn't that she wanted Marie herself, it was simply instinctive to deny others what they wanted. Before the Queen could frame a refusal, Catherine drew out a brooch that Henry had given her. "This is for you, my lady-mother. I hope the King will be even more generous when I bear his child."

Isabel understood the implications at once. Catherine was now the Queen of England, and as such could be very useful.

"Of course you may take her. I would not dream of parting the two of you. She has been your friend since childhood. She will be informed."

Isabel rose and gave Catherine a light peck on her cheek.

"I must instruct the servants to prepare for the journey." She hesitated a moment. "I trust you will be comfortable in England."

It seemed for a moment as if she would say more, but she turned and began berating her ladies for stepping too close to the fine hem of her dress.

"And that is the way I will always remember my mother," Catherine murmured and unaccountably there were tears in her eyes.

–

Marie was constantly sick as the ship tossed its way across heavy seas, and spent most of her time below decks bathing her forehead in rose water; but Catherine felt no ill effects, on the contrary she enjoyed the strange feeling that being afloat gave her. Part of her contentment was the fact that the handsome gentleman with the red hair was among her escort to England. She discovered that his name was Owen Tudor, and that he was a gentleman of Wales; that he was quick of mind, witty and intuitive; in fact, everything she had ever dreamed of in a man. It was foolishness, and she knew it! But all her time was spent in his company, and even now, her ladies were beginning to gossip.

Marie fortunately was too indisposed to notice.

The sun was a crisp clear orb over the swelling seas. Catherine breathed in the fresh air and flung back her head in pure joy. She became aware of the tall figure at her side and the colour rushed to her cheeks.

"Your Majesty." Owen Tudor bent over her hand, his blue eyes looking directly into hers. "Land has been sighted; soon you will set foot on the shores of England."

Catherine allowed him to take her hand, and for a moment she enjoyed the feel of his lips against her fingers. She wanted to fling herself into his arms to beg him to hold her close and teach her the true meaning of love; and for an instant it was as if he could read her thoughts – his grip tightened and he moved fractionally closer to her. She turned from him abruptly.

"It is a great pity that I am the Queen of England, and have a duty to bring my husband heirs. I would much rather be free to choose my future; but instead, it is all mapped out for me."

She glanced up at him, drinking in his tallness, and the young lines of his face, as he stood beside her in the sunlight.

"Do you know what I am trying to say, Owen?"

He stared at her for a long time, and the lap of the waves filled the whole universe, almost drowning them both with its rhythm.

"I know only too well what you are saying, your Majesty, and I will always be your most devoted servant. If you will excuse me, there are some details I must attend to before we land."

Catherine stood silently watching the shores of England draw steadily nearer, and in spite of the excitement of her ladies, and the bustle of activity, the impending landing caused, she had never felt so lonely in the whole of her life.

Chapter Four

"My lady, the King is here!"

Marie's round face glowed with excitement. Her mistress would have ample opportunity to show the cold, arrogant English ladies how quickly she would get with child now that her lord was home.

Catherine rose from her chair, controlling the shaking of her hands with difficulty. She had been expecting Henry for some hours and the strain of waiting had given her a headache. She did her best to act like a joyful wife, but there was only sadness in her heart.

"My lord, welcome home."

She dipped before him, noticing immediately how thin he'd become; his eyes had lines of strain around them, but in spite of everything, he looked every inch a king. His scarlet doublet glittered with gold decorations, and his cloak hung gracefully down from his broad shoulders.

"Well, Madam, have you no kiss for your husband?" He drew her to him, and embraced her. "We will eat, and then I will tell you about my campaigns."

Catherine sat beside him at table, watching him pick at his food with little interest.

"You seem tired, my lord." She was grateful that she could find some genuine feeling for him even if it was merely compassion. "You must rest well before you return to France."

Henry smiled at her rather dryly.

"I'm not an old man yet, my dear lady. Thirty-three is the prime of life, is it not my lords?" He put his arm around Catherine, and drew her close. "I will prove it to you as soon as possible, I *must* have an heir."

Humphrey, Duke of Gloucester, laughed softly. "I envy you, brother; such a task is one of the pleasanter duties of state!" Catherine felt the colour rise hotly to her face, but she sat docile and outwardly calm, though deep inside there was beginning a sensation of trembling despair. She glanced sideways and met the blue, steadfast eyes of Owen Tudor. He smiled almost imperceptibly, and somehow she felt reassured.

At last, the interminable meal was over. Henry rose and held his hand towards her, his stern expression forbidding any of the assembly to make an ill-favoured remark.

Catherine rested her hand on his, and with her head held high she walked along beside him, her heart beating so rapidly it seemed as if everyone must be aware of it.

Her ladies began to help her disrobe.

Henry became impatient and waved everyone away.

"As God is my judge, I believe they would help me with the act itself – if it was possible – or necessary!" He took Catherine's hands and led her to the bed. "Come Catherine, soothe my aching head; and put me in a good humour. I'm tired of war and weary of seeing my men fall sick and die. Help me to forget it all for a short time."

She lay beside him and wound her arms around his neck. He was her husband, and he was distressed; and it was in her power to comfort him in some small measure, and her heart lightened at the thought.

–

Henry was in an ill humour. He paced around the large hall, and then spun angrily on his council.

"Why isn't the money forthcoming? I can't fight a war without arms and provisions for my men."

Humphrey tried to pacify him.

"Times are hard, Henry. The people at home are becoming discontented with the poverty they have to endure." He saw the King's brow tighten, and added hastily, "The money will be raised Sire, have no doubt about that."

It was illogical, but Catherine felt sorry for her husband. He really believed it was his divine right to rule the French throne, and for years he had fought hard only to be frustrated now by a lack of funds. For a moment she harboured a faint hope that now the wars in her country might cease, but then she realised that Henry was too determined a man to give in over such an important issue.

"My lord, may I speak with you? It is a matter of great importance."

He looked at her as if he'd forgotten her existence.

"Ah, Catherine. I will join you in a few minutes; wait for me in your chamber."

For a moment his hand touched hers, almost carelessly as one fondles a dog, but she warmed to him and her smile was brilliant as she left the room.

She sat in the sheets and brushed out her hair. Henry liked her hair: not that he had ever said so, in fact in the four months since his return from France he had never once said he liked anything about her. But in the night, he would smooth out her hair until it spread across the bolster in untidy curls. It was probably his only act of tenderness, but then he wasn't a man for sweet talk – he was a soldier for all that he was a king. She understood him better now and though nothing could make her love him, she was able to reach out and comfort him when he needed her.

"In bed, Madam, are you ill?"

Henry stood in the doorway, hesitating as if uncertain whether to enter or not. Catherine smiled and held out her hand to him, shaking her head.

"No, not ill. I am happy to tell you, my lord, that I am with child. I pray to God it will be a son."

Slowly Henry came towards her, his face lit with joy.

"That is the best news I have heard in a long time, Catherine, my dear queen." He kissed her fingers and looked over her head, out across the green fields, as if seeing things that Catherine could not visualise. "It is a son, and a sign to me that I must redouble my efforts in France, so that my heir will be secure abroad."

Catherine curled her fingers around him.

"Sire, could you not stay at home for a time? You are not well, and surely you have conquered enough ground already?"

He pulled away from her sharply. "You do not realise what you are saying, Madam, or is it that your French loyalties are stronger than your duty to your child?"

Catherine looked down at her hands. "I am French, my lord, and I hate to see my country beaten and in poverty, but the people here are desperate, too. They pay heavy taxes so that they can scarcely live. I am sorry for them."

Henry raised his hand imperiously. "Madam, silence! How dare you seek to instruct me in matters of state? You forget yourself."

Tears spilled over Catherine's cheeks, and her shoulders shook with the violence of her sobs. At once, Henry softened and put his hand over hers.

"You cannot be expected to understand these things. And you are carrying my heir, so you must take great care of yourself. I want you to remove from Windsor for the birth. There is a legend of ill luck, silly no doubt, but I would rest easier if you did not have my son here."

He kissed her fingers and rose to leave.

"I will return to France as soon as possible, Catherine, but for now you must rest and take care of yourself, and my son."

She watched him leave with mixed feelings, and for a moment, as she thought of France, she wished she could go with him; there was no gaiety in England.

"Marie!" she called suddenly. "Come and talk to me. I am lonely."

–

It seemed that she saw Owen Tudor at every turn. He was extremely popular with ladies, and it was obvious that they admired his fine looks and his wit as much as she did. He was bending now over the hand of a dainty, pink-skinned creature, and Catherine felt large and awkward in her full skirt that was designed to conceal her growing waistline.

"Owen Tudor," she said imperiously, "I wish you to walk with me. Women companions can be very tiresome at times." She ignored the astonished glances that followed them, and breathed deeply of the cool air.

"Have you any plans, sir?" she said carefully.

He looked surprised. "Plans Your Majesty? What plans could I have? I am instructed to stay here and attend you, when the King returns to France."

Catherine glanced up at him from under her lashes.

"I meant in your private life, Owen. Have you no wife in mind?"

She held her breath, waiting for his reply. His eyes met hers, and at the look in them her colour rose.

"I have only met one woman I could love, and she unfortunately is quite unattainable."

He smiled with such sadness that she longed to throw her arms around him and hold him close. Instead she looked down at the soft grass.

"I am to have Henry's child," she said softly, feeling in some inexplicable way that she had betrayed Owen.

"It is your duty, Your Majesty, and I am happy for you and the King. May I escort you back to the hall?"

Henry was seated in his great chair listening with pleasure to his musicians; when he saw Catherine with Owen, he lifted his hand in greeting.

"Young Tudor, let us hear some of your wild barbaric singing. Come Catherine, sit at my side. You have never heard anything like this before, I'll warrant."

The Welsh words with their strange cadences melted into the music in a way that enchanted Catherine. She closed her eyes, and allowed herself to dream that the words were a love song to her alone. She imagined herself in Owen's arms, living her life with him, and bearing his children.

She opened her eyes again as Henry touched her arm, and she was once more Queen of England. She rose, excusing herself abruptly, and as she left the hall she heard the tone of the music change; it became happy toe-tapping melodies, and when she glanced over her shoulder she saw that Owen was leading the new, blonde lady-in-waiting into the dance.

–

The preparations for Henry's return to France were almost completed, and it grieved Catherine to think that soon fresh assaults would be made on her country. In the privacy of her bedchamber, she paced slowly to and fro, wondering if perhaps even at this late date she could persuade Henry to delay the attack.

"Please, my lady, let me do something with your hair before His Majesty sends for you. And do sit down, otherwise you will be ill."

Marie bustled round like an old hen, and reluctantly Catherine allowed herself to be led to a chair. She was beginning to feel the discomfort of her pregnancy now, and her back ached intolerably.

There was a bustle of movement among the ladies in the outer chamber.

Marie whispered, "It's the King!"

Catherine struggled to her feet and made an effort to curtsey to Henry. Smiling, he took her hand and drew her to him.

"Take care of yourself, and my son, Catherine. And please make ready for the move in good time. I don't want the birth to take place here, remember that."

He kissed her cheek and then turned away, walking with purpose into the corridor.

She watched from the window as he mounted his horse and led the army of men away from Windsor. The sun struck fire from his sword, and suddenly the sound of horses was ominous like the beginning of a storm when the thunder rolls across the sky. She shivered a little and crossed herself, drawing back into the warmth of the chamber.

–

Outside the sun sparkled, in spite of the cold, and Thomas Cooper rubbed his arm thoughtfully, forgetting that since the battle of Agincourt there had been no feeling in his deadened limb.

"It's a strange sad sight, Tom. I can't help wishing we were riding among the King's army."

Tom looked up, startled to see Owen Tudor standing alongside him. He wondered briefly why the young gentleman was not, in fact, going to France, but it wasn't for the likes of him to question the doings of his betters, and he owed the young man a debt of gratitude that nothing could repay. Why, if it wasn't for the bravery of Owen Tudor, he, Tom Cooper, would be lying still in France, rotted into the foreign soil.

"It is sad at that, sir, and I'm off to drown my sorrows in some good ale. Would you care to come with me?"

As soon as the words were spoken, Tom regretted them. It didn't do to get too friendly with the gentry, even with one as decent as this one.

"Though I 'spects you are more than busy, sir."

He half turned away when Owen spoke.

"Thank you for the invitation. It's the best one I've had in a long time. Courtiers are very fine fellows, but most of them know nothing about war, and it's good to talk over old campaigns now and then."

They sat in companionable silence for a while, and at last Tom drew a map in the spilt ale on the table, trying to reckon how long the journey would take.

"If only I had both my arms strong as they used to be, I'd be with them all the way."

"I think you did more than your share, Tom. Have you settled down to your new duties on the estate?"

Tom liked the open air work, all right, but where was the excitement, the challenge that war had given?

"I like it well enough, but something's missing. You know how it is?"

Owen suddenly became serious, "Oh, yes, I know how it is all right. I should be riding out with the King, and instead I stay at home with the Queen. I'm worried, because I want to stay behind if the truth be told."

Tom looked at him closely. "It seems to me that I worry too much about the past, and if you don't mind me saying so, sir, you worry too much about the future." Owen threw some change on the table and walked out into the crisp air.

"You are quite right Tom. But if a man hasn't dreams, he has nothing. And now I think it's time I was getting back."

The two men walked in silence both occupied with their thoughts.

–

"I'm ugly, oh! Marie, look how ugly I've become."

Catherine pressed her small hands against the swell of her stomach where her red velvet dress rucked into folds that were meant to conceal. Marie clucked her tongue in exasperation.

"I've never heard such nonsense in all my life. Your skin glows; and look at the shine on your hair! Your bosom has filled out too," she said craftily. Catherine looked down at her breasts consideringly. "And usually the figure is much improved after childbirth."

Marie broke off a thread with her teeth and examined the tiny garment she had just finished sewing.

Catherine laughed. "How is it you know all this, Marie? I don't see you with a brood of children round your skirts."

Marie shrugged. "Oh, I've helped with a good many deliveries. You know how good I am with my remedies, my lady."

"There is only one remedy for me, and that is time. Already I feel as ripe as the fruit in autumn." She seated herself with difficulty and gasped at the pain in her back. "Soon I must face the effort of moving. I am not looking forward to that in the least. I've grown to like it here." Marie stared at her thoughtfully. "You are carrying the child very low, my lady. I wonder if the birth is nearer than it was first thought?"

Catherine drew a deep breath. "I am most uncomfortable in this stupid chair. I know that much. It obviously wasn't made for pregnant ladies." She struggled to rise. "Help me to bed Marie. It might be better if I lay down for a while."

Deftly Marie helped Catherine to undress. A worried frown appeared between her brows, as she helped the Queen into bed.

"Don't look like that, Marie. I'm all right, but do try to keep those silly ladies from me, especially that little blonde one. I sometimes wonder if she deliberately sets out to irritate me."

Marie smiled indulgently. "It's just one of those strange feelings expectant mothers get. Jayne is quite a nice girl, really, once you get to know her."

Catherine closed her eyes. "Jayne, plain Jayne," she murmured, but unfortunately it wasn't true! The girl was very pretty, in an English sort of way, and Owen Tudor seemed to be in her company a very great deal. "I'll try to sleep, Marie."

Catherine yawned and turned carefully on her side. The bed was soft and comforting to her aching body, and it was good to relax.

It was dark when she woke and someone had placed a candle near her bed. Grotesque shadows leapt along the walls and Catherine turned over on her back wondering what had disturbed her. Then it came, the fingers of pain crushing her bones and pulling strongly at her stomach.

"Marie are you there?" she said urgently. She heard the sound of someone moving in the adjoining room and then Marie came and stood beside the bed, her face rosy from sleep.

Catherine struggled to sit up.

"The baby is coming," she gasped. "It is too soon. And I am still at Windsor. What will Henry say?"

Dimly, she heard Marie issue instructions that the King's brothers be sent for, and the physician brought from his bed.

"Lay quietly my lady. Everything is going along nicely, just as it should. And a baby will come when it's ready, not when it is a convenient time."

Suddenly the chamber seemed to be blazing with lights. The women scurried around with bundles of linen, and Marie held out a cup for her to take.

"Drink it my lady. It will ease the pain." Marie's voice was the only comfort that Catherine wanted, but obediently she drank and sank back on her pillows wishing the frightened ladies to the devil.

Gloucester, his hair ruffled beneath his hat, lifted his hand in salute to her. "God be with you, sister, that you may give my brother the son he deserves."

Catherine searched for the face she most wanted to see, but Owen Tudor was not there. Tears came to her eyes as another pain gripped her and she heard from outside the soft haunting notes of a Welsh love song, and she knew that he was there.

She almost screamed as the midwife and physician made themselves busy beneath the sheets.

"It won't be long now," Marie said comfortingly, "the head is almost born." Catherine managed a fleeting smile before she gave herself up in total concentration to the birth of her child.

Chapter Five

The keen January wind howled outside the thick walls of Windsor Castle and played ghostly music through the long corridors. Catherine whimpered and moved restlessly in her sleep. A log fell in a shower of sparks, flaring for a moment and illuminating the sleeping figure of Marie, her sleeves still rolled above her plump elbows and her hair escaping in untidy tendrils from her hat.

Catherine opened her eyes and stared uncomprehendingly at the crib, and then tried to sit up. She gasped as a pain gripped her.

"Marie," she said softly, but immediately the girl was awake and crossing the room on tiptoe.

"I have a pain here. I thought all discomfort ended with the birth. Help me sit up, Marie." She relaxed a little as the pain subsided. "Bring me the baby, Marie. I want to hold my son."

Marie smiled indulgently. "I'll bring him, but make the most of it; once those starchy English nurses get their hands on him they won't allow him to be disturbed from his sleep." Gently she lifted the tiny boy and placed him in Catherine's arms. "He's a bonny child, my lady. His Majesty, King Henry, will be so pleased and proud."

Catherine's smile faded. "He will be angry with me for giving birth to his son at Windsor. I should have made the move sooner, but I confess I was reluctant to leave. I have been so happy here."

She looked down at her sleeping son and her eyes misted with tears. His skin was petal-soft against her cheek, and his hair was downy and fair, lifting up from his head in little tendrils.

"It was a good thing you hadn't started the move; you might have given birth to the King's son out in the fields!" She busied herself with some herbs diffused in water, straining the liquid until it was quite clear. "This will help with the pain, my lady. It is probably afterpangs, and will not last long."

The baby stirred and opened his eyes. His small fists fought the wrappings that bound him and waved futilely against the air. His lips quivered and he began to cry, softly at first, and then with growing force.

"Oh, Marie something's wrong with him. What is it my little love? Are you in pain?"

She didn't protest as Marie took the child from her and began to rub his back.

"Wind my lady, that's all it is," Marie said smiling.

Slowly the pale sun was coming up, dimming the candlelight and dispelling the mists that wreathed the castle.

"You must try and eat something, my lady," Marie urged. "Soon your visitors will come to look at the new prince. The bells will ring out the good news, and the citizens of the town will flock around bringing gifts. You must be strong to face it all. Here, have some of this good thick soup. It will warm you all through; then perhaps some duck, or even a pie."

Catherine held up her hands in protest. "Some soup is all I can manage for now, thank you, Marie. I promise I won't allow myself to waste away, but really I'm not very hungry."

75

She tasted the soup and found it delicious, and as Marie had said it warmed her and brought some colour back to her cheeks.

"Your Majesty." One of her ladies was at the door, her dress billowing like a flower as she curtsied to Catherine. "The Duke of Gloucester is asking to be received. Shall I show him in?"

Catherine, her mouth full of soup, nodded and waved her hand indicating that he be brought to her at once. She would be happy to see him. He had been delighted that the prince was strong and healthy, though for a moment there had been something almost like jealousy in his eyes as he'd looked down at the sleeping infant. Still that was only human. As brother to the King, he, no doubt, entertained the faint hope that he might himself one day rule England.

"My dear Catherine, you are looking so well and more beautiful than ever." Humphrey kissed her cheek, avoiding her eyes, and she knew at once that something was wrong.

"What is it Humphrey? Have you news of the King? Is he coming home?" Catherine waited in suspense as Humphrey studied the ruby ring on his hand, struggling desperately to find the right words.

"The King is ill, Madam, and that being so I trust you will forgive the sharpness of his letter to you. He is upset because you did not leave Windsor sooner; but he conveys his pleasure that you have born him a strong heir, and he indicates the wish that the boy be called Henry."

Catherine inclined her head, in agreement.

Humphrey shifted his position. "You had better read the letter, Madam; but try not to worry yourself too much. My brother has spent a bad winter. The siege of Meaux has seriously taxed him; let us pray it is nothing more than that." He rose, and bowed over her hand. "I will leave you to rest now, Catherine. Look after yourself and my little nephew. And don't take Henry's letter too much to heart."

As soon as he had left, Catherine unfolded the heavy document and Henry's writing bold and angry leapt out at her. Her colour faded as she read the harsh angry words he had written – to him she was nothing less than a traitor for disregarding his wishes. She dropped the letter, and stared out at the cold bleak landscape. She had never had much of a marriage, but after this how could she bear to continue an alliance that was obviously so distasteful to the King?

"What's wrong, my lady? You look like someone bewitched. Is there anything I can do?"

Marie bustled around the bed pulling the covers in place and straightening the pillows. Catherine shook her head listlessly.

"I knew the King would be displeased, but I didn't think he would take it so badly. He assumes I stayed here deliberately to flout his authority." Catherine bit her lip in an effort to stop the tears. "He should have remained with me as any loving husband would do, and then he would know it wasn't my fault."

Marie shook out Catherine's foot rug with undue vigour, her actions revealing her indignation, but she knew better than to voice any criticisms.

"Please rest my lady," she said with forced calmness. "You must be given time to recover your strength."

-

The bells that had rung out so joyfully only a few short months ago to celebrate the birth of a prince, now tolled mournfully on the warm, still air proclaiming to the people that their king was dead. Catherine sat in her favourite corner of the grounds draped heavily in dark mourning clothes, and there were tears on her cheeks. She cried because Henry was her husband, and the father of her child, but she felt no real sense of loss.

"Try not to grieve, Catherine. My brother would not have wished it." John of Bedford patted her arm almost paternally, though he was no more than a few years her senior. "As regent, I will look after my nephew's interests as if they were my own. You need have no fears on that score. And when I leave for France, you will have Humphrey to protect you here."

She put her hand out to him in gratitude. "You are very kind, John. I don't know how to thank you."

She thought with pity of the tears that had sparkled on his brown cheeks as he'd ridden with her behind the coffin, and how the crowds had cheered to see her. It had come as a surprise to realise that she was so popular in England, partly, she guessed, because she had provided them with a new king. And she was living proof of French submission.

"I will miss your sense and kindness very much, John. I will pray that the wars will soon be finished, and then you may be here to help with my son's education. He needs someone like you to guide him." She leaned forward on an impulse, and kissed John's cheek. "And God go with you, my lord."

He flushed with emotion. "And God be with you, Catherine. Guard the infant king well. While he lives there will be no fight for power. He is the sovereign, and there can be no disputes."

Catherine felt a chill of fear at his words. As she watched him stride away across the grass, she felt an impulse to call him back and force him to stay at home to care for Henry himself. But she knew with a deep certainty that he would not give up the struggle for France any more than her husband would have, and one day the effort might kill him as it had killed the King.

–

"Why should the magnates oppose my wish to be Regent?"

Humphrey paced the great hall, his colour high and his arms waving angrily and Catherine seated in her high chair could not help feeling a measure of sympathy with him. "Do I not guard the young king and his mother, and do I not love my country?"

His voice rose dramatically and one of the ladies sitting behind Catherine giggled softly. "Yes and does he not love the ladies too well," she whispered.

Catherine silenced her with a look and Humphrey came to stand before her.

"Can you think of any reason, or cause, that could go against me, Your Majesty?" he asked.

She smiled up at him sympathetically. "Perhaps they will relent, my lord; and for myself I could not hope for a better Regent for my son and myself." She set out deliberately to charm him out of his ill humour. "Come Humphrey, let us call out the musicians. Music will soothe and entertain us."

She saw Owen Tudor enter the hall, and immediately her heartbeats quickened. To hide the blush that rose to her cheeks she smiled ever more warmly at Humphrey.

"Perhaps I can put in a word for you, my lord; though I doubt if there will be much notice taken of what I have to say."

He suddenly took her hand and raised it to his lips. "You are the most sympathetic and charming woman it has ever been my fortune to meet."

He looked into her eyes, his own hot and searching. Catherine disentangled her hand, feeling slightly uneasy.

"And you, my dear brother, are the most flirtatious of men, with a gift of charming the ladies that is second to none. Do you not think to add me to your necklace of pearls!" She laughed to soften the reproof, but the speculative look remained in Humphrey's face.

She stayed a little while longer and then making the needs of her infant son the excuse, left the hall.

She had been resting only a few minutes when her ladies entered.

"Your Majesty, Duke Humphrey of Gloucester wishes to see you."

Catherine swallowed a sigh, and sat up reluctantly.

"Very well, show him in."

She folded her hands together in an attempt to look composed, but Humphrey was quick to notice the traces of tears on her cheeks.

"My dear, you are unhappy. But that is only natural with my brother only recently buried." Humphrey took her hand folding it between his large fingers. "But you must not be lonely. I will not have it, and isn't it a natural thing that I your kinsman should wish to comfort you?"

He smiled, and looked so young and handsome that Catherine warmed to him.

"Your kindness is very much appreciated, I assure you. I will take great pleasure in your company, as I have always done. But tell me now, what is the real reason you were not allowed to be Regent?"

Humphrey stood abruptly, and Catherine realised that she could not have found a more effective way of diverting him than the one she'd chosen.

"My uncle, the Bishop of Winchester, is my real enemy. He desires to become a cardinal. He is power mad, but then the Beauforts were always ambitious."

Catherine was surprised by the bitterness in his voice. "But, my lord, no one is more powerful than you and John of Bedford, the young king's very own uncles. Who could usurp your authority?"

Humphrey patted her hand. "The Bishop is rich, very rich; and wealth speaks with a loud mouth in England today. With money, he controls a great deal of the country's affairs, and continues to line his pockets as well. But don't worry about it; we will talk about more pleasant things."

Long after Humphrey had left, Catherine thought about what he had said. It was becoming increasingly clear that there were plots afoot that she had no knowledge of and no control over. She sighed. Humphrey wasn't quite the pleasant, if amorous fool, she'd imagined him to be. He wanted power as much as anyone, and she wondered to what lengths he might be prepared to go to get it.

–

News came through from France that Duke John was doing well in the campaigns. It pleased Catherine to learn that instead of leaving desolation behind him across the country, he was making new laws to help the people rebuild their lives.

"You are looking very thoughtful, my lady. Is anything troubling you?"

Marie stood before her mistress, her cheeks flushed from the walk she had just taken, her hair tossed by the wind.

"I wonder if anyone remembers me at home now that my poor father is dead?" Catherine said. "I expect my mother is already consoling herself with a new lover. They will be more eager than ever to win her favour now I daresay. And Charles, will he ever forgive me for that treaty that gives my son precedence over him for the French throne?" Catherine covered her eyes. "I feel as if I've been a pawn all my life, Marie; used by other people to bring them something they wanted. I've never been loved for myself alone."

Marie tutted, overcome with emotion. "Don't take on so, my lady. You have always had my love."

Catherine looked up quickly. "Oh, I know how sincere your devotion is, Marie, believe me, I didn't mean to hurt your feelings." She sighed. "I'm afraid that Humphrey is intending to ask for me in marriage. He hasn't spoken of it, yet, but only because I've managed to keep him at arm's length. He wants power. As my husband and step-father to the King, he would be the most powerful man in the country." She leaned forward resting her chin on the ledge. "If I was sure a man loved me for myself alone, even if he were a commoner, I'd take him for a husband."

Marie looked shocked. "My lady, don't even say such things. You were brought up in a royal household, the princess of France, and now you are Dowager-Queen of England. You could not think of marrying beneath you."

Catherine looked at her with tired eyes. "I may not be an honest woman and marry but I can be like my mother and take lovers when I choose. Is that what you mean, Marie?"

Marie shrugged in bewilderment. "I suppose you could marry suitable to your rank, my lady. There are many of the lords who look to you with more than a passing interest."

Catherine got to her feet suddenly throwing a cushion to the floor. "I'm sick of doing what is acceptable to other people. I am flesh and blood! I do not stop feeling just because I am Queen Catherine of England."

She ran to the bed and fell across it sobbing hysterically. She longed more than anything to confide in Marie about her love for Owen Tudor, but she would never understand how a queen could love a gentleman-at-arms.

He was drifting away from her. She had seen him yesterday talking intimately with the simpering lady Jayne, and if she wasn't very much mistaken the girl was with child.

–

"My father will never agree to me marrying you and when he finds out about the baby I will be in disgrace. He will disown me."

Jayne looked up at Owen, her blue eyes large and filled with tears; and he wondered what on earth had possessed him to make love to her.

"Come, don't cry. There must be some way out of this. Surely if I explain to your father how it was, he will forgive you, and allow me to provide for the child?" He took her in his arms. "I don't like to be unkind, little Jayne, but I wasn't your first, nor your only one was I?"

She didn't answer, just burrowed her face closer to him, hiding like a little animal from the unpleasant facts of the world.

"We will make an appointment to see Her Majesty Queen Catherine and throw ourselves on her mercy. There is no other way."

Jayne was suddenly frightened. "I can't face them all, Owen."

"Yes, you can. It's time you faced reality Jayne. There are unpleasant things. But I'm with you and I'll protect you. Don't worry."

–

The Queen was pleased to give them an audience, but she requested that they wait in the outer chamber until her other business was finished.

"She does it to humiliate me," Jayne whispered fiercely, and turned to outstare one of the many ladies who seemed to find pressing errands that took them to and from the chamber.

Owen felt there was some justification for her feelings, and as the time went by, his own anger began to grow. Several of the courtiers came through, and one of them made a lewd remark; then Catherine appeared for a moment in the doorway of her chamber, her eyes sweeping over Jayne as if she were some sort of curiosity.

Suddenly Owen rose. "Your Majesty!"

His voice echoed along the length of the corridor startling everyone into silence. He walked determinedly to the door of the chamber.

"Your Majesty, do we have an audience with you or am I mistaken? If I am wrong and you do not wish to see us do I have Your Majesty's permission to retire?"

Catherine studied him coolly for a moment, her dignity unruffled. "You may enter and bring the Lady Jayne with you. And you have my assurance that I am not deaf or stupid. And I will not be shouted at in my own castle."

The very control in her voice showed the strain she was under, and suddenly Owen's anger left him as he saw the dark shadows that circled her eyes, and the paleness of her cheeks. She waved her hands to the ladies who reluctantly left the room, disappointed at having to miss the excitement.

Catherine went to her chair and seated herself. "You may say what you have come to say. And Lady Jayne please be seated."

"Your Majesty, my apologies for causing a scene. I did not mean any disrespect." He bowed over her hand and her eyes did not flicker. "I have a problem,

Your Majesty. I do not know quite how to explain it."

Catherine's eyes rose to his for a moment. "I can see that," she said coldly, "but you will have to try won't you?"

He stared steadily at her. "Jayne is going to have my child," he said abruptly, and before he could continue Catherine held up her hand.

"If you are seeking permission to marry the lady, the answer is no! I have already arranged a betrothal of which her father approves." She turned to the trembling girl. "Run along; my ladies will inform you further."

With a quick look at Owen, Jayne hurried away thankful to have escaped so lightly. Catherine rose from her chair and stood before Owen, staring closely into his face.

"Do you love her?" Her voice was edged with anger, and he lifted his eyebrows in surprise.

"No. I do not love her; neither does she love me. You know where my affections lie, Your Majesty."

Catherine clenched her hands together. "Affections? I don't think you know the meaning of the word. How could you associate with the lady Jayne if your love is given elsewhere?"

"I am no saint. I am a normal man with desires and needs, and Jayne is very attractive. It was no more than that. If it hadn't been for the misfortune of her getting with child, the affair would have passed unnoticed."

Catherine struck his chest with her small fist. "I would have noticed," she said, her voice low with anguish. She moved closer to him, resting her hands on his sleeves. "Owen, Owen, how could you?"

She was so close he could see the fineness of her cheekbones beneath the creamy skin. He felt almost dizzy, and instinctively his arms closed around her even though he knew he was committing treason. She leaned against him, raising her lips so that they met his, and they were full and sweet filling him with an aching tenderness that he had never experienced before. She drew away.

"Please leave me," she said, and her mouth was soft and trembling with desire, and her dark eyes overflowed with tears.

Chapter Six

Henry Beaufort, Bishop of Winchester, sat in his high-backed chair facing the open window. It pleased him to contemplate his vast estates, especially at times like this when he needed reassurance. His parchment-dry hands shook as he twisted them together. He could still hardly believe that an attempt had been made on his life. He reached reluctantly for the goblet of wine placed discreetly at his side, by his manservant.

He was quite aware that he had made more than one enemy in his life, especially since his nephew Henry had died in France, after some of the most brilliant military campaigns in the whole of the long war. With the King a mere child it was inevitable that a battle for power should be waged around the throne.

He relaxed a little as the wine began to take effect. There was no shred of doubt in his mind that

Humphrey, Duke of Gloucester, was the instigator of the scandalous attack. His hate for his uncle, the Bishop, was common knowledge, but that he would go to such lengths to be rid of him was quite amazing. He made a sour face as he contemplated Humphrey's popularity. The people loved to see him abroad with a new woman on his arm every week, shamelessly parading his lust for everyone to see.

"Good Duke Humphrey!" they shouted as he passed by, his face reddened by drink and his very soul a pit of corruption. There was a whisper now circulating among the members of the Court that he was making a play for the hand of the Queen. Not at all dismayed by the fact that she had been his brother's wife.

He rose from his chair and leaned from the window. The grass, soft and green, stretched as far as the eye could see, and he breathed a sigh of contentment. It was good to be one of the richest men in England. Wealth brought power; it would certainly buy anything, even men. Many of the powerful councillors were in his debt, and by clever scheming he meant to keep it that way. He paid them well for their attendance at meetings, and yet some of the scoundrels had taken Humphrey of Gloucester's side against him.

The wine was making him feel sleepy. He left the chamber and called to his servants.

"I would rest a while, but have a man guard the door every second, so I may lie easily in my bed."

He turned to the bedchamber, a frail elderly man, mumbling angrily to himself.

"There is no gratitude left in England."

–

"My lord, welcome back to England. It is good to see you again." Catherine smiled warmly as John of Bedford bent over her hand.

"You look well, my lady. Time is indeed a great healer. I only wish it were more pleasant business that brought me here."

Catherine frowned. "Ah, the attacks on your uncle the bishop." She studied John. He was a wise and sensible man. If anyone could settle the quarrel it would be him. Humphrey respected him and listened to his counsel and so apparently did the wild Duke of Burgundy, in France.

He took her arm. "How is the young king? Well, I hope?"

Catherine glanced around the hall. Among the courtiers there would doubtless be spies planted by both Humphrey and the Bishop.

"Would you like to walk outside, Madam?" John smiled, rightly interpreting her look.

The grass was soft beneath their feet and even though some of the ladies had followed Catherine they respectfully kept their distance.

"I hardly see Henry now," Catherine said softly. "Not that I'm complaining, my lord. I realise he must be brought up to be manly and know his duties as king." She paused for a moment. "It's just that when I do see him, he seems weak and indecisive even for a boy as young as he is. I feel he needs more encouragement to make decisions."

She shrugged her shoulders.

"One of the gentlemen used to take him out a great deal, teaching him to hunt and ride. But Humphrey put a stop to it. He said it wasn't fitting that a Welshman should tutor the King of England. And yet, young Henry had a great affection for Owen Tudor."

John took her hand. "Don't worry, Catherine when I return from France for good, I'll be able to care for the boy and teach him myself."

"Yes, of course, my lord."

She knew she had failed. John was a good man and could not be aware of the bad influence Humphrey had on the young king. And then there was the Bishop pulling him in the opposite direction. Both of them trying to mould the child into a pattern that most suited their own ends.

"And what about you, my lady? Have you no plans for your own future?" John asked the question so suddenly that Catherine was startled.

"In which way do you mean, my lord?"

"Well Catherine, you are still a young woman. Wouldn't you care to marry again?"

Her heart began to beat painfully fast. "I suppose I would like to marry if the right person came along, but you know, my lord, that for a queen the right person is difficult to find." She attempted a laugh but her mouth was dry.

"I hear that Humphrey has been paying you a great deal of attention lately. Is it possible that you would consider him for a husband?"

"I don't think I could consider that possibility, my lord," she said quietly. She thought the matter would end there, but John persisted.

"Then there is no one who holds your particular affection?"

She clasped her hands together, twisting them nervously. "I have no lover, if that's what you mean."

John smiled indulgently. "There is no need to be on the defensive, Catherine. I am not an irate father, and it did not enter my head that you would be so indiscreet." He walked a few paces ahead. "I merely wondered if it would be advantageous to both of us if we made some alliance. You are a lovely girl and forgive me, a valuable piece of merchandise with which to bargain." He shrugged apologetically. "I'm only saying what many of the lords are thinking."

Impulsively, she put her hand on his arm. "Leave it for a while, my lord. You have so many problems on your mind that I, and my affairs, are the least of your worries." She whirled around. "Let us return to the others, or they will soon find something else to talk about!"

She went immediately to her chamber. The talk of marriage had disturbed her, though she was forced to admit that John of Bedford spoke excellent sense. She was still young, and her four years of widowhood had been a trial. She was not the daughter of the hot-blooded Isabel for nothing. She sat at the window, her head in her hands. If Henry had lived things would have been different. She would probably be mother to a brood of children by now.

Then there would be no time for this foolish and misplaced longing for the Welshman. Her face burned beneath her fingers, the relationship between them had changed subtly after she had married off the foolish girl he'd got with child. She remembered with an almost physical pain the shock he'd given her, shouting out so that his voice echoed along the corridors. He was so strong in his righteous indignation, and so handsome that she'd almost given in to the temptation then to take him as her lover. She wondered why she had not yet done so.

"My lady." Marie tiptoed into the chamber. "The Welsh gentleman is outside. Shall I send him away?"

Catherine sat upright as if stung. "No!" she said sharply. "I wish to see him."

Owen came quietly into the room. "Your Majesty." He bowed over her hand, and glanced at

Marie, waiting for her to leave. Catherine dismissed her with an impatient wave of her hand.

"What is it?" she asked, staring up at Owen almost fearfully. He looked unusually serious and so very masculine in the femininity of her chamber.

"Your Majesty, will you allow me to leave Court?"

"Owen." Her voice was soft, and she held her hands towards him, forgetting that she was the queen. "I cannot let you go away from me."

As he took her hands, she leaned towards him and they clung together in silence for a moment.

"I love you, Owen. My life would have no meaning without you."

Tears trickled down her cheeks, and he kissed them away tenderly.

"It is impossible, you know it better than I do." Unable to help himself, he kissed her lips, and for Catherine this was the moment in her life she'd always waited for.

"We must be allowed to marry," she said softly.

He drew away, looking into her face in astonishment. "They would never permit it! Humphrey wants you for himself. And John would have you make an advantageous marriage."

Catherine lifted her head proudly. "They don't own me. They can't make me marry anyone. I will approach the council." Her eyes gleamed suddenly. "The Bishop may help. He would do anything to thwart Humphrey. And he is very influential, if only for the reason that most of the council owe him their livelihood!"

Owen held her hands tightly. "You must not take risks. They could be very difficult over this."

He was troubled. Catherine was impulsive, she may regret her decision when she'd had time to think things over.

"Allow me to go to Wales," he said, "and if you still feel in the same mind when I return, I will make the necessary arrangements."

Catherine clung to him. "Please Owen, don't go. I need you here with me. Please!"

He held her close, unable to resist the pleading in her eyes. "All right Catherine I'll stay. But remember I'm just a man, and when I hold you in my arms, you are not a queen, but a woman."

He kissed her passionately and she clung to him, carried away by a wave of emotion such as she'd never experienced before. She held his face in her hands and drew away gently.

"We will have a most marvellous marriage, my love. Be patient for a little while longer."

It was becoming the talk of the palace, the way the Welshman was constantly seen in the company of the Queen. Marie sat in the evening light, struggling to see the fine sewing on her knee.

"I don't know what things are coming to," she said as she threw the needlework down impatiently, and crossed the room.

Through the open door she could see Catherine surrounded by her ladies, throwing back her head and laughing as if she were a child again. Before her stood the Welshman, apeing the fine, extravagant gestures of the English courtiers. With a flourish he bent over Catherine's hand, and Marie could see that he was inviting her to dance. She curtsied low and took his hand, and both of them capered in the flickering candlelight before the horrified stare of the ladies.

Marie tutted crossly, and shaking her head, walked away from the scene. Her mistress was making a spectacle of herself. There was no doubt about it. Maybe if she spoke to her lady she would be more discreet.

"Ah Marie, why are you standing here almost in darkness? Can it be you are in love?"

Catherine sounded so light-hearted that Marie could barely summon courage to speak.

"I was thinking, my lady." She turned to Catherine. "I can see how happy you are, but is it right for you to behave so?"

Catherine turned a dull red. "What exactly do you mean?"

"They are talking about you. Those cold English ladies laughed behind your back, and call you Isabel the Second. I'm sorry, but it had to be said."

Catherine stared for a long moment, and then turned on her heel. Marie could hear her shouting and berating everyone in the chamber and then there was silence. Marie went cautiously towards the doorway. Catherine was lying in a heap on the floor, her shoulders shaking as she cried soundlessly.

"Oh my lady!" Marie hurried forward and helped Catherine to her feet. "Come to your bed; rest a little, you'll feel better soon."

Passively the Queen stretched out on her bed. "If I can't have him for my husband, I want to die," she whispered.

"So the Queen wants to see me."

The Bishop of Winchester allowed himself a moment of triumph as he folded the letter and placed it carefully in a cupboard. He had been seeking a way to influence her in his favour and now it might just be that his chance had come.

"William old friend, she wants something. And if I can provide it I will," he smiled, craftily.

His companion felt a little sorry for the young queen. Once in the Bishop's power, it was more than difficult to escape.

"Congratulations, Henry." The dryness of his tone was disguised by his smile. "I hope you will accomplish what you wish."

The Bishop's face was enigmatic. "I usually do, William."

–

Henry Beaufort bent as low before the Queen as his rheumy back would allow him. "Your Majesty, how can I be of service to you?"

Catherine made an attempt to smile warmly.

"Come we will walk a little." She glanced around at the ladies who were forever with her. "I wish to speak privately. Surely you can trust me alone with a Bishop!"

The ladies dropped back a little sheepishly, but then they were exactly like sheep, following someone or other's orders and not caring a jot about their queen.

She glanced at the man at her side. He wasn't really so old and yet everything about him gave the impression of age. His hands, like dry branches of a tree and his sparse hair showing a little under his bishop's hat, seemed to belong to a man well past his prime. It must be the dry-as-dust life he led, she concluded.

"My lord Bishop, there is a matter I wish to consult you on."

"Anything I can do, Your Majesty, I am more than willing to help you."

Encouraged by his amiability, Catherine relaxed a little. "I wish to marry again," she said quickly.

The Bishop raised his eyebrows and nodded. "Quite understandable of course. I don't see where you need advice, however. Surely you are free to marry if you wish?"

Catherine shrugged. "In this case, I don't know. The man was a gentleman-at-arms to my husband Henry; and what's more he is Welsh, which seems to prove some kind of barrier."

The Bishop sucked in his cheeks. "Do I understand you to be talking about Owen Tudor, the one Humphrey has taken such a dislike to?" He walked a few paces in silence and Catherine's hopes rose at the gleam of amusement in his eyes.

"Can you help me?" she asked breathlessly.

The Bishop deliberated for what seemed an eternity before answering. "There is more than one way of skinning a cat," he said at last. "I will speak to the council, Madam. I have some influence with them, as you probably know. We will see what can be done." He sucked in his cheeks again. "I take it that you will virtually relinquish your duties of looking after the young king then?"

Catherine stared at him steadily. "I will not give my son up entirely, but I will naturally make known my preferences of adviser to him."

The Bishop nodded thoughtfully. "I will see what can be done, Your Majesty."

Catherine watched him leave with mixed feelings. She had chosen her time well. Humphrey was away from Court and John of Bedford had left once more for France. No doubt both would be informed of the Bishop's visit, but by then he would have spoken to the council, and if she read him correctly would have influenced them in her favour.

She went slowly into the palace and made her way to the royal apartments. The ladies stared at her, resenting her presence, but in the absence of any other authority they could not stop the Queen visiting her own son.

Henry was with his tutor, patiently going over and over his words. He was small for his five years, his eyes blue and anxious as they looked up at her. Her heart melted as she put her arms around him.

"I hope they are not working you too hard." She looked pointedly at the young man who persisted in staying at the table with the King. He bowed his head but did not move. Catherine took Henry's hand and led him to the door.

"Your Majesty, I have my instructions." The tutor bowed, frightened by the ferocity of her anger.

"My instructions are that you keep out of my way. My son is coming outside into the fresh air.

He needs some colour in his cheeks. He is still only a child."

She swept out of the room, and docilely, her son accompanied her.

"Come Henry. We will look at the flowers, and play in the lovely soft grass. Perhaps we will go and see the horses, and you may ride a little."

Henry looked at her doubtfully and suddenly tears came to his eyes.

"I'm afraid of horses. Don't make me go on one."

She looked down at him with pity and took his hand in hers. He didn't resist. He went with her passively, the tears rolling down his cheeks.

"My poor boy," she said softly, "between them all they are making a weakling of you."

She drew him into her arms and he curled up like a small soft animal, his head leaning wearily against her.

For a long time she sat in the grass holding her son, knowing that with her decision to marry Owen she had forfeited her few remaining rights over her child's future.

Chapter Seven

"The Council has betrayed me!" Catherine stormed through her chamber, clenching her fists to her sides to prevent her from striking out at someone. "In spite of the Bishop's promise of help, an injunction has been made forbidding the marriage without the King's consent. Consent!" Catherine's voice was contemptuous. "How can a small boy give his mother consent?"

Marie hurried into the room. "My lady, please don't take it so badly. You will find a way. Everything will come out all right. Don't cry so bitterly." She rubbed the Queen's wrists, struggling to keep the tears from her own eyes. "Decisions can be revoked; you know that as well as I do."

Catherine sat up and held her hand wearily to her temples. "They think they have beaten me, Marie," she spoke rapidly in French so that no one could understand. "But they don't know Catherine de Valois very well. This is one thing I want more than life itself, and I will do anything in my power to bring the marriage about."

From outside the door came sounds of voices raised in argument, and Catherine indicated that Marie go and find out what was the cause of the disturbance.

"It is Owen Tudor, my lady. He wishes to see you, but the ladies are attempting to send him away. He is very unpopular since the rumour about the marriage spread around; many of the courtiers have taken to ignoring him."

Fresh anger brought Catherine to her feet. "I will see him, but in public; and if anyone dares to slight him they will have me to answer to."

She refreshed her face with the sweet orange water that Marie quickly prepared, and then dressed carefully in her most magnificent gown.

"Give me your arm Owen. I wish to join the company."

Gracefully she moved along the corridors to the great hall, smiling into Owen's eyes assuring him without words of her unchanged love.

Humphrey rose from his chair as she entered, and bowed politely. "I had heard you were indisposed,

Your Majesty, but I am greatly relieved to see that it is not so. You look more beautiful than ever."

She favoured him with a brilliant smile. "My lord, it is a mystery where these tales come from." She waved her hand including the elegant courtiers in her conversation. "Boredom causes a great deal of mischief, don't you agree?"

As Humphrey made to move away, she caught his arm tightly. "I have asked Owen Tudor to entertain us with his singing. It is my wish that you remain in my company for a time, my lord, so as not to offend such a worthy friend of the throne." She smiled warmly at Humphrey. "But of course, you know how he fought with our late king at the battle of Agincourt; how many here have so fine a record I wonder?" Some of the lords looked to Humphrey for direction.

"I'm sure that while he maintains his high record of obedience, no one would wish to offend Owen Tudor, Your Majesty." He thrust the words from him as if they burned his lips.

Catherine inclined her head. "I trust you are right, my lord, because he who does so, offends the Queen of England, and that could be called treason, could it not?"

She relaxed her hold on Humphrey's arm and he withdrew, his colour high and his eyes dark with anger.

"He hates me like poison!" Owen whispered. "Be careful that he does not become your enemy, too. He is a formidable man and would stop at nothing – even murder – to gain what he wants."

"Let us forget them all." Catherine waved her hands in the air as if to sweep her worries away. "Sing me some of your lovely Welsh songs, so that I can dream we are in a different world with all our problems solved."

She seated herself comfortably in the high-backed chair in the centre of the room, and closed her eyes as the haunting melody filled the hall.

–

Marie heard the singing from the solitude of her chamber. The notes filled her like liquid gold, and suddenly she was filled with an unbearable longing – a longing for something that she couldn't explain. She looked down at herself wondering how much she had changed from the young girl who had lain in the sweet fields under the moon with young eager Michel. It wasn't that she had grown old. Her body, though a trifle plump, was still well-shaped and attractive. But somehow the cold English climate, and even colder Englishmen, had robbed her of her laughter and gaiety. She needed a man to love her, to make her bloom again.

She heard the bustle of the ladies' dresses in the royal chamber, and then her lady's voice called her name. Marie smiled. Pushing back her discontent, she hurried to Catherine's room. The Queen was lying on the bed, her dress a pale flower against the richness of the tapestries that hung around the walls.

"I see you are recovered from your mood, my lady. Have you put a few noses back where they belong?" Marie smiled indulgently as Catherine rolled over on to her stomach, and kicked her slippers on to the floor.

"Oh, yes, and the biggest nose of all was that of the Duke of Gloucester. He didn't take it kindly. But he was forced to be polite to Owen. Of course, all the others followed like the sheep that they are." She sat up and crossed her bare feet under her skirts. "All the same, they think I am tied by their wretched injunction, but the Bishop will find a way I'm sure of it. He longs to be a cardinal and will go to any lengths to achieve his ambition. What's more, he hates Humphrey; it's common knowledge."

Marie stood hands on hips. "Be careful, my lady. Humphrey is a clever and powerful man. It wouldn't be wise to underestimate his capabilities."

Catherine nodded. "I know. But he will be very careful, because one day my son will be king."

-

The dawn crawled greyly in through the palace windows, resting pale fingers on the bed where Catherine lay already wide awake. News had come from France which had disturbed and frightened her, and at the same time aroused a strange excitement within her.

Her brother, the Dauphin, had decided to go to war with the English, led it seemed, by a maid they called Joan. Victories were being won as town after town was recaptured for France, and this woman, who paraded shamelessly in man's clothing, had so inspired Charles that he was contemplating a coronation some time in the near future.

That meant defeat for John of Bedford, and the loss of the French throne for her son; but nevertheless, the events held some satisfaction for Catherine. With her brother crowned as Charles the Seventh how much stronger her own position would be. Even Humphrey would be forced to recognise Charles, and perhaps he would urge the council to withdraw the injunction forbidding the marriage.

Impatiently, she pushed the sheets aside and padded on bare feet to the window. The stone was cold to her touch, and she shivered, thinking of the mellow sunkissed walls of the palaces in France. It was a great pity that Owen would not consider living abroad. There were so many places more pleasant, and much safer than England. The pale sun rose and splashed patches of light across the fresh spring grass, and Catherine breathed deeply. If the truth were known, she too would grieve for England if she were forced to leave it now.

Her ladies were astonished when they saw she had risen without calling on them.

"I wish to go out early and take a walk in some pleasant company," she declared arrogantly, knowing quite well they would disapprove.

"Your Majesty demeans herself." The voice was small but decisive, and Catherine stared in astonishment at the lady Mary Beaufort who knelt at her hem arranging her petticoats.

"What did you say?" She gave her skirts a sharp tug so that the girl almost toppled over on to her knees. She curtsied and got to her feet.

"I think you should have more consideration for yourself and your position, my lady."

Mary Beaufort was a good few inches taller than the Queen, and though her hands trembled she was obviously determined to have her say. Catherine, even in her anger could not help but admire her courage.

"I presume you are talking about my affection for Owen Tudor?" She spoke almost pleasantly, aware that the other ladies were waiting with bated breath. Lady Beaufort nodded, her lips pressed firmly together. Catherine faced them all. "He was a friend of my late husband, the King. Is he not good enough then to be my friend?"

The silence stretched uncomfortably and even Mary Beaufort avoided the Queen's eyes.

"Very well," Catherine said briskly. "I have not taken him to my bed, so what is it you object to?"

Mary Beaufort stepped forward and Catherine noticed that her eyes were narrowed spitefully. "We could understand that, Your Majesty, but to even consider marrying a – a Welshman!"

Catherine recoiled at the scorn in her voice. Her eyebrows rose and she waited for an explanation.

"I beg Your Majesty's pardon, but such a man is lower than the most common English yeoman. The Welsh are a most barbaric race."

Catherine spoke quietly. "I see no difference of face or stature except that he is of better build than most Englishmen, and being myself a foreigner, I was not aware that there was any difference of race in these British Islands. I have been indulgent long enough. I will hear no more. Continue with my dress so that I can take advantage of the sunshine while I may."

She was not to have her walk. Already the courtiers stood in little groups in the corridors, and the name of the Maid of Orleans was on everyone's lips. Catherine moved towards Humphrey.

"Surely a woman is not capable of outwitting the English army?" She spoke with concern. She knew that the Duke firmly believed in the young king's right to rule France.

"Unfortunately, Madam, that is just what she is doing."

"I should not take it all too seriously," she said. "John of Bedford is an experienced soldier. He will know how to deal with the situation."

Suddenly she was at a loss not knowing what she wanted. If Charles was the victor, her son would be cheated of the French throne; and yet her brother was entitled to rule in his own country. He, too, was the son of a king.

With relief she saw Owen enter the chamber. He looked very handsome in the morning light, every inch a man with an aura of virility that was almost tangible. She went to him and laid her hand on his arm.

"Come and talk to me. Lighten my spirits!"

In the shadows of the corridor, Owen drew her aside and held her close, kissing her lips and hair. "Catherine, you are so beautiful," he murmured, and her hands shook as she pushed him aside.

"Tempting though it may be to stand here and enjoy your embraces, we must walk in full view of all at Court. I will not be labelled whore, as my mother was."

Sedately, she walked along the stones, and Owen fell into step beside her. She longed to take him to her chamber and close the door on the outside world. She wanted nothing more than to lie in his arms and enjoy his love; but not yet – everything must be perfect between them.

"My ladies tell me you are a barbarian, because you are a Welshman. Does that make you angry, Owen?"

Something she could not understand forced her to hurt him. He stood still and looked down at her, his face pale and his blue eyes unwavering.

"They may say what they wish, but I want to know what you think of me, Catherine."

He was motionless, and suddenly she was sorry for the strange impulse that had taken possession of her. She put her arms around him, but he did not return her embrace.

"You know what I think, Owen. I long to marry you and be your wife; and have your children. Could I say all this unless I loved you?"

"Half of the court are of mixed blood, mine is pure. Come down to me from the great princes of Wales. I am proud of my heritage, Catherine, and I want you to be proud, too."

She lifted his hand to her lips. "I love you Owen. I am proud of you." She stood on tiptoe and kissed his lips until at last his arms held her close.

Out of the corner of her eye, Catherine saw the flutter of a dull brown gown and sighed. Lady Mary Beaufort was hurrying at full speed to catch her attention. She drew herself up and took a deep breath. Let her dare to speak any more treason and she would be punished.

"A messenger came from the Bishop, Your Majesty." She was breathless, and her eyes were wide with curiosity as Catherine took the document from her hand.

"Why were you entrusted with it?" Catherine spoke sharply, her heart beating rapidly with hope that the Bishop of Winchester had found a solution to her problem.

Mary curtsied. "The Bishop is my kinsman, Madam. Had you forgotten?"

"Do you know anything of the contents?" Catherine persisted.

Mary looked exasperated and shrugged her square shoulders. "I know nothing, Your Majesty, except that I must keep the matter of the letter a close secret."

Catherine broke the seal and quickly read the Bishop's spidery handwriting. A smile came to her lips, as she passed the letter to Owen.

"You may leave us now; and thank you for the service you have done me. I will not forget it."

Mary hesitated for a moment hoping Catherine might say more, but the Queen turned away and there was nothing she could do but curtsey and leave the royal presence.

"Well, Owen, what do you think of that?" Catherine's eyes glowed. "The Bishop feels that a secret marriage would achieve our ends. There will be nothing Humphrey or anyone else could do once the ceremony is actually an accomplished fact."

Owen was suddenly serious. "Catherine, I couldn't love you more than I do now." He looked at her intently. "Why marry me at all, and risk so much? I would be content with anything you were prepared to give."

Catherine held both his hands. "That is not for us, Owen, haven't I said that time and time again? I want a real marriage, and I have waited a very long time for real love to come into my life. I won't have it made a shoddy thing, unsanctified by God and the church. Can't you understand, Owen, I want to be your wife."

He drew her close, and Catherine rested her head on his shoulder. Her eyes closed, oblivious to the courtiers who looked the other way pretending not to see their queen and the Welshman close together in an embrace.

Chapter Eight

"Marie, come quickly. You won't believe what has happened!" Catherine was so excited she could hardly speak. "Charles has been crowned King of France. It's true, the ceremony took place yesterday in the cathedral at Rheims!"

She sank down into her chair, her hands clasped together, making a crumpled ball of her handkerchief, as she pictured the scene. The hot July sun would be spilling through the magnificent stained-glass windows, and the jewel-bright clothes of the courtiers would set off the old, mellow stones of the cathedral walls to perfection.

"I wonder how Charles looked, Marie. If only I could have been there to see him anointed with the holy oil; with the princes and bishops waiting to acclaim him their king. Oh! how wonderful it must have been!"

Marie moved uneasily. "My lady, the Duke of Gloucester is waiting outside. He begs an audience with you; and the young king is with him."

Catherine rose hastily and hurried into the outer chamber, brushing the tears from her eyes and doing her best to still her shaking hands. She curtsied quickly to her son and then leaned forward to kiss him.

"I beg your pardon for keeping you waiting. The news from France has so disturbed me. And how are you my lord duke?"

Before Humphrey could reply Henry placed his small hand on his mother's arm. "It really doesn't matter if your brother rules France, Mother," he said innocently. "I don't really wish to go there to live anyway. I like it here in England."

Catherine flushed aware of Humphrey's displeasure. "Please, let us be seated and we shall have refreshments brought to us. We might as well be comfortable while we talk."

Henry smiled warmly at her, and she longed to hug him, but she doubted if Humphrey would approve of such a gesture.

"John intends to deal firmly with this insult, of course. It cannot be allowed to pass, you realise that?"

Humphrey was becoming just a little arrogant. He looked at Catherine speculatively, as if she was one of his women; his eyes probed as if they could see through her clothes, and Catherine felt her anger rise.

"Are you aware that your tone is not one usually used to address the Queen of England?"

She spoke quietly but two spots of colour burnt in her cheeks. Humphrey collected himself and bowed quickly.

"I beg your pardon, Your Majesty. It is just that like you I am upset that a usurper has taken the throne from our sovereign." He waited while Catherine inclined her head in agreement, and then continued: "I believe that John intends for the King to be crowned in Paris, but the details are not yet complete."

Catherine glanced at him anxiously. "Is it safe, my lord? The King is so young." Unconsciously her hand came to rest on that of her young son, and with a smile Henry curled his fingers into hers.

Humphrey leaned forward. "John would do nothing to endanger such a precious life, you know that as well as I do, Catherine."

She nodded. She believed implicitly in John's integrity and wisdom.

Without warning Humphrey spoke softly. "Perhaps now you will forget these foolish notions about marriage that you have been harbouring. There are more important things worthy of your attention at the moment."

Catherine avoided his eyes feeling a momentary panic. He did not know, he could not, that a plan had been devised already for her to travel to Wales, there to be secretly married to Owen. She glanced at him from under her eyelashes.

"You are right, my lord, there is certainly a great deal to think about just now, and talk of marriage to anyone is just idle speculation. It may be that my brother, Charles may ask me to go to visit him in France. Surely negotiation with him is a possibility?"

Humphrey put his hand over hers. "Every eventuality must of course be considered. And who could speak more persuasively for the King than his mother?"

Catherine sighed with relief, thankful to have diverted the conversation away from marriage. She smiled warmly at Humphrey, her eyes large and free from guile.

"Perhaps a short retirement from social occasions might be of benefit. I would like time to be alone and to reconsider my feelings on several issues."

She allowed him to press her hand to his lips, and continued to smile up at him.

"My dear Catherine, that is an excellent idea. A few weeks at one of the country houses would be most beneficial to your health. I could join you in a few days, and in that way put paid to any gossip-mongering. Just decide where you will go, and leave me to make the arrangements."

He rose and bowed over her hand once more. "I'll look forward to our next meeting Catherine." He turned to Henry. "Your Majesty, are you ready to accompany me?"

Henry reached up to kiss Catherine's cheek and her eyes misted with tears as she held him close for a moment.

"Be good, my son, and God go with you."

Her eyes were still blinded by tears so that she did not notice for a moment that it was Mary Beaufort who stood within the royal bedchamber placing rose water in a bowl at the side of the bed. The girl dropped into a swift curtsey, but not before Catherine had seen and understood the smirk that played around her thin, bloodless lips. She was a spy and would watch the Queen's every move, and no doubt report faithfully back to Humphrey.

Catherine smiled to herself as she waved her hand in dismissal. Marie would have to make herself busy with one of her special potions. Mary Beaufort looked tired and would be all the better for a good long sleep.

–

Marie sat at the bottom of the swaying boat, her stomach sick and her head dizzy. First there had been the terrible journey through the soaring Welsh mountains that had caught and held the wind until it howled like a live creature in torment and now, worst of all, the trip by sea with nothing but this tiny boat to carry them. Her bones ached intolerably, and yet the Queen seemed to feel none of the discomforts: on the contrary, her skin and eyes glowed as if she was enjoying every minute of it.

The boat ground to a halt on the shingle, and thankfully Marie stood up listing unsteadily on legs that seemed reluctant to obey her.

"Here, let me help you, though I'm afraid my days for lifting fair maidens are over. I leave that sort of thing to my lord Owen Tudor."

The man holding out a hand to Marie smiled indulgently as the Queen of England was carried up on to the shingle away from the lap of the waves.

"Ready?" Owen's voice rang out firm and clear against the lap of the waves. "It's not much further, I promise you. Then we shall have some good food and wine to revive us."

Marie looked up at the man, and he put his arm around her.

"Come along. A young girl like you should think lightly of small discomforts. Hang on to Tom Cooper. I've one strong arm to support you."

He laughed and Marie laughed, too, in spite of herself.

"Flatteries can be very sweet, but I must say you pick a fine time to utter them. All the same, I'll remember your words, and if I have the opportunity, I may encourage you to repeat them!"

Suddenly the little group were halted by the appearance of a man dressed in a monk's habit, and Marie's panic subsided as she saw Owen Tudor greet him as a friend.

"Come," the man said softly. "The lady Elizabeth is ready to receive you."

Marie sighed with relief when she saw the flickering lights gleam through the windows of the large grey building. The huge polished doors were flung wide, and there was a small dark lady drooping gracefully before the Queen.

"Welcome, my home is honoured by your presence." She spoke to Catherine, but Marie saw that her eyes never left the face of Owen Tudor. He moved forward and kissed the lady's cheek.

"Elizabeth, it is good of you to open your house to us. We are both very grateful." He draped his arm carelessly round the lady's slender shoulders and Marie saw at once how it was. Elizabeth loved Owen Tudor.

Catherine was not slow to notice it either. She moved towards the great hall, her head erect and her mouth pressed into a firm line.

Marie stood for a moment watching her mistress's straight back. It was strange how similar, from a distance, the two ladies were, and towering above them both, Owen Tudor walked easily like a man on familiar ground.

"Come along, it seems a meal has been prepared for us." Tom Cooper took Marie's arm and drew her away from the hall. "Can't you just smell that roast meat?" His eyes met hers and suddenly he was serious. "I've known Owen Tudor since he was a young boy of no more than fifteen years. We both fought at Agincourt, along with the old king. You've no need to worry about Queen Catherine. She will be happy with him, I've no doubt."

Marie stared ahead. "It is a great step for anyone to take, but in these circumstances things can go so terribly wrong. What if the young king is persuaded to take his revenge on Owen Tudor? What will happen to my lady, then?"

Tom Cooper pressed her waist. "You worry too much, and the journey has taken all your strength. Let us eat and refresh ourselves. With something warm inside you, you will soon be more cheerful."

Marie smiled reluctantly. He was a good man, this Tom Cooper; strong, with rugged features and bright eyes – a man to bring some excitement into a woman's life.

"I hope I will be seeing more of you in the future, Tom," she said coyly. "I hear you are joining the household?"

She placed her hand in his and smiled as he nodded. He didn't need to speak, the eagerness in his face said it all.

—

The great bedchamber seemed damp and chilly and Marie piled more covers on the Queen's bed. Catherine was quick to feel any change in atmosphere, and it wouldn't do for her to sleep badly on the eve of her wedding.

"Ah, Marie, you have certainly made the bed look inviting. I must confess that at last I am tired."

Catherine looked anything but tired. Her eyes sparkled and her cheeks were warm and glowing, and Marie guessed that a prolonged goodnight kiss had taken place outside the chamber door.

"The lady Elizabeth is in love with Owen, of course. And who could blame her?" She snuggled beneath the sheets, her eyes large as a child's peered at Marie. "I'm surprised she allowed him to slip through her fingers and leave Wales in the first place.

"In the morning, Owen will be my husband, and then nothing anyone can do will alter that." Catherine choked on the words, tears rising to her eyes and Marie felt moved to make some gesture.

"My lady, I don't know how to say this, but I pray you will be happy in your marriage."

She stopped, the words seemed inadequate. But Catherine smiled and Marie knew that she understood.

It was still dark when one of the Welsh servants shook Marie gently awake. Holding the candle high, the small, dark-haired girl gestured that it was time to go. They could not understand each other's words, but smiles and nods were all that was required.

Catherine was already dressed and several ladies were in attendance on her. Their lovely hair, thick and dark, on their shoulders, speaking in soft strange words, obviously delighted by the whole thing.

"Well, Marie, how do I look?"

Catherine's face was pale above the rich green of her dress but her eyes shone with happiness and excitement, and Marie caught her breath overcome by the emotion of the moment.

The ceremony was simple, and dawn was just beginning to spread its warming fingers throughout the tiny church when Owen Tudor and the Queen of England were joined together in holy matrimony. Marie could not help but think of the other marriage. Henry had been a noble and fitting husband for the daughter of the French king, but now Catherine had something more precious than honour; she had love perhaps for the first time in her life.

Tears filled Marie's eyes as the priest spoke the final words and she noticed that the lady Elizabeth had difficulty in composing herself.

"Come, Your Majesty," she said, her voice husky, "I have prepared a small celebration in honour of the occasion." Her eyes flew to Owen's face. "I wish you every happiness, from the bottom of my heart."

Owen bent forward and kissed the lady Elizabeth's cheek. "Thank you for everything, my dear; nothing can ever express our gratitude."

Catherine took Owen's arm and with an effort added her thanks to those of her new husband.

"We will be delighted to join you in any entertainment you may have planned," she said, though it was obvious to Marie that she would sooner have been left alone with her new husband. "Please, Lady Elizabeth lead the way; today is a time of merrymaking, and I want everyone to be as happy as I am this moment!"

–

"It's a beautiful country after all. I admit it now that I am not forced to cross it at breakneck speed."

Marie sat carefully on a rock that was warmed by the sun, climbing higher now in the bowl of the sky. Tom stood at her side, his hand shielding his eyes as he looked out across the water.

"It's lovely, all right, but give me the soft fields of England any day." He crouched down beside her and took her hand. "It's a sad pity that we've not got to know each other before this. I wonder how such a mishap came about?"

Marie looked boldly into his eyes. "I don't know, but you're certainly not wasting any time now, are you?" Tom laughed and slid his arm experimentally around her waist. "I was one of the swiftest archers in the King's army. Now, isn't that a nice firm waist; not too skinny, something for a man to get hold of." His eyes crinkled with laughter as Marie slapped his hand away. "Spirited too; that's just how I like them."

Marie pretended to be indignant. "And I suppose there have been so many that you couldn't count them! Well you are not adding me to your string, my lad!"

When he replaced his arm she pretended not to notice, staring across the waters of the straits, as if deep in thought. Tom put his face close to hers.

"Now that we are to work together, I think you might be a little bit more friendly."

His lips brushed her cheek, and as she turned to rebuke him his mouth was on hers, firm and surprisingly exciting.

"I'm not difficult to get to know," she said breathlessly, "but there is no need to rush into the attack quite so quickly."

She pushed him, and he toppled over into the damp grass, laughing heartily. She lifted her skirts and hurried back to the big grey house, her heart beating rapidly. It seemed that some of the Englishmen had blood in their veins after all.

–

Catherine lay languorously beneath the sheets. At her side, Owen stretched his tall frame and his bare thigh touched hers. Immediately she felt a renewed response and turned to him, her lips warm against his.

"Owen, my love, I have never been so happy in the whole of my life."

There were tears on her cheeks as she wound her arms around the warmth and smoothness of his shoulders. He drew her close against him, kissing her in slow deliberation so that they could both savour the moment.

"Love me for ever, Owen," Catherine whispered, as her eyes closed in delight.

Later, she rested against the bolster drinking deeply of the wine Owen had placed beside her. She would have slept, except that the lady Elizabeth had sent an invitation for her to join in the musical entertainment in the great hall. She had sent Owen on before her and he had looked so handsome in the rust-coloured doublet that almost matched the colour of his hair, that she had wanted to call him back at the last minute.

She stretched luxuriously. There would be ample opportunity for them to be alone together, for now it was only paying a debt of gratitude to appear to enjoy the events the hostess had arranged for them.

"I have brought you some rose water, my lady," Marie said as she appeared in the doorway smiling like the cat that had swallowed the cream. Her plump cheeks were pink and her hair was falling from its cap.

Catherine sat up oblivious to the fact that her small firm breasts were exposed. "What have you been up to, Marie? It looks as if you are the bride instead of me."

Marie laughed. "Not quite that, my lady; but I have met someone I feel I could love. His name is Tom Cooper, a servant to your lord."

Catherine laughed and flung her arms over her head. "Good! If he follows his master, you should have something to look forward to!" She slipped from the bed. "Bring me the water, and I think I will wear the red dress; it is Owen's favourite." She felt as excited as a child, as Marie helped her to dress. "Oh, Marie, if only I could have done this years ago. Look at the time I've wasted!"

Marie stood back to survey her handiwork. "My lady, you are more beautiful now than you ever were at fifteen."

It was the truth! Catherine was like a rose that had come to the peak of its beauty.

Chapter Nine

It had rained steadily since they had left the mountainous regions of Wales behind them, and Marie felt the dampness chill to her very bones. A far cry, indeed, from the hot sunshine she had taken so much for granted at home in France. Still, the journey had not been too unpleasant, for all the discomfort, because Tom Cooper kept her constantly aware of his presence. She turned to smile at him and he answered her look with a saucy wink. She sighed; it would not be long now. Soon they would be within the walls of the magnificent mansion the Bishop of Winchester had put at the Queen's disposal. There would be hot meat and good wine, and no doubt enormous fires to take away all the aches that came with the rain. Yes, the worst of the journey was now over.

Wales was as beautiful as Owen Tudor had claimed, but give her the hustle and bustle of the

English court any day, in preference to the primitive loveliness of the Welsh hills.

And yet the Queen had loved it all. Embracing the countryside and enveloping it with her love – as she enveloped her new husband.

Marie smiled as she caught a glimpse of Catherine's face almost hidden in the fur of her hood. She was radiant with happiness, just as a bride should be. And there was a fresh youth and zest about the Queen that Marie envied with all her heart.

One of the forward riders called out that the mansion-house was in sight, and Marie rubbed her aching back, uttering a prayer of thankfulness. Soon the small party was riding through the arched gates. The Bishop himself was waiting to greet them, standing with his hands folded piously, and a smile almost of amusement on his face as he glanced at Owen Tudor.

"Welcome to my humble home, Your Majesty. I will do my best to make you comfortable."

Marie, taking her mistress's private boxes to the chamber, smiled to herself. If this was what the Bishop thought of as 'humble' he must indeed be as rich as everyone said he was!

The bedchamber was enormous, with tapestries thick on the walls and some even spread about the floor. To Marie, it seemed sinful to have such beautiful possessions underfoot and carefully, she walked around them, placing the Queen's jewel box in a cupboard near the bed.

Everywhere she went, there was a curious perfume, heady and sweet, freshening the air. It certainly seemed a wonderful thing to be a bishop.

Behind her, Marie heard a slight sound. She turned suddenly and saw someone in the shadows, half hidden behind the drapes.

"Come out whoever it is. I won't bite!" Her voice was sharp, with an edge of fear to it; there was something about the Bishop that Marie did not trust.

There was a swish of skirts and the sound of a door closing, and Marie was alone. She shrugged; probably just some inquisitive maid, trying to catch a glimpse of the Queen. All the same, she held herself alert, glancing over her shoulder occasionally; but no one came again.

—

Catherine smiled across the table at the Bishop. His dry hands plucked at the food, without interest, and she knew that he had more important things on his mind. She decided to put him out of his anxiety.

"My lord, I have been wondering how best to thank you for your help and kindness to me."

She toyed with the brilliant goblet filled with ruby wine and pretended to consider the matter. She looked up and caught the gleam of avarice in his eyes, but knew it was not money he wanted. He had more than enough already.

"I have some power in the church," she said casually, "though, of course, I do not dictate in any way where religious matters are concerned. However, I may recommend a course of action."

She glanced at Owen, and he lifted his brows, quite well aware of what she was doing.

"If I were to suggest that the position of cardinal would be no more than you deserve, would you be prepared to take on the additional responsibilities, my lord?"

She did her best not to laugh as the Bishop of Winchester almost visibly rubbed his hands in delight.

"Your Majesty, I am deeply honoured," he said, already picturing himself in his cardinal's robes.

Catherine rose. "If you will forgive me, my lord, the long journey has tired me. I will retire."

Her eyes flashed once more to Owen, and he gave a hardly perceptible nod as Catherine crossed the large hall. The Bishop didn't even notice Owen leave. He was standing before one of his magnificent stained glass windows recently bought at great expense from an Italian craftsman. He saw nothing of its beauty. His thoughts were more concerned with power.

Owen walked along the corridor, bowing as he passed a young woman who for some reason held her hand up to her face. He shrugged, smiling; he was the last one to pry into the affairs of others.

—

"But I saw him, my lord, with my own eyes. Owen Tudor went brazenly into the Queen's bedchamber!"

Lady Mary Beaufort was almost ill with excitement; her face was pale with tiny beads of moisture on the bridge of her nose, and the Bishop turned away in distaste. He had been foolish to have the girl here at such a time. He'd forgotten that she was one of the Queen's ladies.

"Keep your own counsel about this, child," he said sternly. "The Queen's affairs are her own."

"But Uncle Henry, the Queen was in her night attire. They must be very intimate to see each other like that."

"You are ill advised to say such things, madam! You know nothing of the facts of the case, nothing at all."

Mary's lip quivered. She knew her uncle well. He seldom stepped out of his role as benign kinsman; it was one he enjoyed playing. She allowed a tear to tremble on her cheek.

"I'm sorry, uncle, I didn't mean to offend you. It's just that I was so shocked. I always thought of the Queen as virtuous."

Henry patted her hand. "You were right to come and tell me. It could prove embarrassing if this got out; but it shall be our little secret." He delved deeply into a cupboard and drew out a sparkling necklace. "Here, this will help dry your tears, child."

"Thank you so much, Uncle Henry. It's beautiful."

She held the gems up to the light, and they sparkled like fire. It was worth a great deal of money, and she fully understood that it was a bribe to keep her mouth shut. But about what exactly?

He waved his hand, excusing her, and she hurried from the room jubilantly clutching the necklace. If her uncle, the Bishop, was prepared to pay her to keep quiet, there were others who would no doubt pay for information. All she must do now, was consider the best way of finding out exactly what that information was.

-

"Ah, a man after my own heart. You really care about the animals, I see."

Tom Cooper looked up in surprise from his task of grooming the horses that were to carry the royal party back to Windsor. The lady standing smiling down at him was no beauty, but she smiled pleasantly enough, and she was right; he *did* care about the animals.

"Did you want a horse, my lady? Shall I bring one out for you?" he asked politely, though it was no part of his duties to care for the demands of the Bishop's household.

"That's very kind of you. I'm a bit nervous, so choose a docile creature."

She did, indeed, seem nervous. Tom helped her into the saddle after several unsuccessful attempts and he had taken advantage of the situation to hold her a little more tightly than strictly necessary.

"I must be very stupid," she said, breathlessly, "but I was ill as a child, and not allowed to ride very much."

She seemed reluctant to move away from the stables, and Tom felt it would be oafish to walk away and resume his work.

"Is there any way I can assist you my lady?"

"Oh, if only you would be so kind as to ride a short way with me?"

She looked at him helplessly, and he was afraid she would become unseated any moment and end up in the mud of the stable yard.

"But, my lady, I don't really think I should. Haven't you a kinsman to ride with you? That would be a more fitting arrangement."

"I have only my Uncle Henry, and he's too old to get up on a horse these days." She smiled to herself. She could almost believe herself that the Bishop was a harmless old man. "Oh, come on. It's very early.

I just want to try a short ride. We'll be back before anyone misses you."

Tom looked across the fields. The early morning mist was swirling like ghosts in the trees, and the air was spicy and fresh.

"I'll come, my lady, but I really must be quick."

Marie had searched anxiously for Tom for what seemed an age. The Queen wished to ride in the pale sun of the early afternoon, and in the end Marie had been forced to bribe one of the Bishop's stableboys to bring horses round to the big door.

Luckily, no one had noticed his absence, but now that Marie was left alone to her thoughts, she racked her brains for a reason for Tom's apparent disappearance.

"You wait Thomas Cooper!" she said fiercely. "If I find you with one of the kitchen maids, I'll have no more to do with you!"

Her voice rang out in the empty room, and feeling foolish, and angry with herself as well as Tom, she went to the window and stared out.

For a moment, she thought the Queen and Owen were returning from their ride already. Then she realised that the man on the horse was not a gentleman in fine clothes, but Tom. The lady at his side wore a rich pink gown, and though Marie could not see her face there was something puzzlingly familiar about her.

"Oh, mother of God preserve us," she gasped. "It's that bitch of a Beaufort girl. If Tom has talked, Humphrey of Gloucester will know about the marriage so fast that my lady will be powerless to prevent it."

–

Tom stood shame-faced before Catherine. "I didn't know who she was, my lady. She seemed so innocent."

Catherine paced about the room, trying desperately to think of something to do. She waved her hand at Tom.

"Don't reproach yourself. You men are notoriously simple when it comes to a pretty face." She stopped still for a moment, and patted Tom's arm. "Aye, and I suppose she put on a pretty good act." The colour stained the man's cheeks, and Catherine felt sorry for him.

"You may leave us; don't worry too much. It was bound to be discovered sooner or later." She turned into Owen's arms as Tom closed the door. "I'd have preferred it to be later on, so that we may have had a few months of peace."

Owen kissed her tenderly. "Soon you will be full with my son; and then the world *will* know."

Catherine laughed and pushed him away. "We are only just married, my lord. Even you must give nature a chance." Owen caught her up in his arms, and carried her to the bed. "I think I will give nature a chance now."

Catherine struggled for a moment. "Owen, we have serious problems to consider. Humphrey, Duke of Gloucester – he will be so angry about the marriage."

Owen held on to her and slipped his hand into her bodice.

"There is nothing he can do. You are the Queen of England." He kissed her, passionately. "And I am your husband, and I love you, Catherine."

With a sigh of pleasure, she relaxed in his arms, stretching her small body in an ecstasy of abandon.

"Owen, you must tell me some time how you have become so adept at giving joy."

She wound slim arms around him, and pulled his lips down to hers.

Marie plodded angrily across the coarse grassland bordering the Bishop's estates.

"Tom, you big fool. I'll warrant that no man would have got the information from you with red hot pincers; but just let a woman smile at you and hand out some favours, too, no doubt, and you open your mouth as wide as a baby chick seeking a worm!"

Tom stopped walking, and leaned against a tree.

"You can't make me feel worse than I do already. I've made a proper mess of things, haven't I?"

He looked so much like a dejected child that Marie's heart softened in spite of her anger. She went to him and reached up to ruffle his crinkly brown hair.

"Ah, well, don't feel too badly about it. I suppose it would have come out sooner or later. It's not the kind of thing that can be kept secret for long." She kissed his cheek. "Come on, don't sulk. What's done, is done! and there's an end to it."

Tom's arm immediately closed around her, his hand fumbling for her bodice. She gently slapped him, but her eyes were soft.

"There is no time for any of that. We are to make for Windsor soon. I've already packed away the best of the Queen's jewels. I suppose we will make an early start in the morning." She began to retrace her steps. "She misses her son, poor little mite. To a king at such a tender age must be a trial. If only he had been grown up, things would have been so different."

Tom took her arm, and matched his steps to hers.

"Yes, different indeed. The Queen would be too old to think of marriage, and come to that, so would we." He looked down at her. "I think I could do worse than take you for my wife."

Marie threw back her head and laughed. "It may be an odd proposal of marriage, but I'm going to accept it before you change your mind."

Later, as they walked back through the grounds of the mansion-house, Marie caught sight of Lady Mary. She was dressed for travelling, and was accompanied by several of her uncle's servants. She saw Marie, and recognised her at once, but looked disdainfully away.

For a full five minutes, Marie stood in the middle of the path and cursed in rapid French until the lady went pale and wheeled her mount sharply away, frightened and superstitious because she had not understood the words, only the hatred on Marie's face.

"That will send her on her way with something to think about as she runs to Gloucester with her tale!" Marie said, as she took Tom's arm, and calmly continued on the journey just as if nothing had happened.

—

The Queen was more beautiful than ever, and though he had spent his entire life practising his own ideas of celibacy, the Bishop could not help admire her radiance and charm. Her husband, like the wild barbaric fool he was, cavorted around her, enticing her to dance. She laughed and tried to wave him aside, but he scooped her up in his arms as if she was a doll, and called out a tune in his strong, clear voice.

He moved further into the hall, and though the Welshman's eyes continued to sparkle, he set the Queen on her feet, and she made an effort to control her laughter, as she welcomed the Bishop.

"We will leave for home in the morning, my lord," she said a trifle breathlessly, "but we thank you most earnestly for all your hospitality."

She sank down and fanned her rosy cheeks.

"Tell me, my lord, is the lady Mary Beaufort still here?"

Henry raised his brows and pursed his lips.

"She left suddenly this morning, Your Majesty. She gave no reason, but she has been told nothing of consequence – not by me, I assure you."

Catherine inclined her head. "I know that, my lord." She smiled graciously. "One of my servants unsuspectingly told Lady Mary, and I feel she is probably on her way to Windsor by now."

The Bishop sucked in his cheeks. "But for what reason, Your Majesty?"

He saw Catherine's impatience, but knew she would play the game out in his way.

"She has always had a fondness for Humphrey; and after all, he is her kinsman, as indeed he is yours, my lord."

The Bishop nodded his head sagely, as if the whole thing had suddenly become clear to him.

"It is unfortunate. The news might have come better from yourself, Your Majesty."

Catherine stared at him, smiling in reluctant admiration. He was a wily old fox!

"The danger now is that he may have a reception committee to see that my husband meets with an unfortunate accident. You see our difficulty, my lord?"

He did, only too well! Hadn't he, the Bishop, been at the receiving end of Humphrey's viciousness some time ago? "I do see, my lady, but what can I do to help?"

He hoped it would be nothing too energetic or demanding. He needed all his strength to see to his own affairs.

"Send a message to Lady Mary," Catherine smiled sweetly. "Tell her we will arrive at first light in the morning." She leaned forward. "That isn't too difficult, is it?"

He was surprised. The Queen was more perceptive than he'd imagined. He bowed as well as his old bones would allow.

"I will send a messenger immediately, Your Majesty."

-

The cloth around the horses' hooves muffled any sound they might have made, and in the pale moonlight their steaming breath gave them a ghostly appearance.

Catherine was enjoying herself enormously and found that she could ride with ease dressed as she was in boy's clothing.

"Who would recognise the Queen of England now," she laughed breathlessly.

Once out into the open countryside, they could give the horses free rein; and Catherine followed Owen, laughing with delight, and struggling to speak against the force of the wind.

"Let them all wait for us at Windsor in the morning. By then, we will be safely settled in at the Royal Manor House. And not even Humphrey will dare to disturb us there!"

The sound of the horses' hooves mingled with happy beat of her heart, as Catherine rode forward towards her new life.

Chapter Ten

"How I hate this English rain. It gives me bone-ache!"

Marie peered out of the window at the sodden landscape, her cheerful face giving the lie to her words.

Catherine eased herself into a chair.

"You think you've got worries; just wait until you feel the discomforts of childbearing, then you'll have something to grumble about."

She smiled happily, hoping that the child kicking so vigorously inside her would be the son that Owen so badly wanted.

"Your Majesty."

One of the ladies was bowing low to Catherine, her eyes, sharp and curious, as they rested on her swollen figure. So far, none had dared question her about her relationship with Owen, though speculation was rife.

"Yes, what is it, Anne? Speak up."

Catherine found it increasingly difficult to control the moods of irritation during her pregnancy, and the veiled hostility of the ladies was like a constant pin-prick to her.

"The Duke of Gloucester wishes to see you. Shall I admit him?"

Catherine made a wry face. "Yes. Tell him I will receive him now."

In spite of herself, her hands trembled. This was the first time she'd seen Humphrey since the marriage.

He bowed formally. "I hope I am welcome in Your Majesty's new residence?" he said coolly.

She inclined her head, and indicated that he should sit beside her. He had changed in only a few months. His face had grown more dissolute, and the firmness of his jaw was marred by folds of flesh that bulged over his collar.

"Joan the Maid has been captured," he said abruptly, and for a moment, Catherine stared at him in amazement. This was the last thing she'd expected him to say. He saw her bewilderment. "The Frenchwoman, Madam, who tried to take away your son's heritage."

Comprehension dawned, and Catherine wondered why Humphrey thought the news so important that he brought it himself.

"We will recapture our rightful lands now, of course," he said and leaned back, fat and self-satisfied, in the chair.

"And the Dauphin? Is there any news of him?" Catherine was almost afraid to ask.

Humphrey smiled scathingly. "He still styles himself king – but not for long."

So, he still held the power! Charles had not lost his following, although the girl Joan was taken.

"What of Joan? What will become of her?" Catherine felt pity for the brave French maid.

"Naturally, she will be given a fair trial, once the Duke of Burgundy hands her over to us."

"Ah, the duke."

Catherine knew that Phillip would demand a high price for so rich a prize; with him, money and power were twin ambitions.

"He is on our side." Humphrey was obviously stung by her lack of response.

"My lord, the Duke of Burgundy will remain 'on *your* side', just so long as it suits him, and not a moment longer."

Humphrey coughed uncomfortably. "In any event, she is taken, and that's the end to the matter."

The interview was not going at all as he had planned. He meant the reins to be firmly in his hands, but Catherine was still every inch a queen, in spite of her obvious pregnancy.

"Henry must go to France – as soon as it can be arranged, of course."

And now, thought Catherine, we come to the real reason for the visit.

"Naturally, we would need Your Majesty's consent to the journey."

He stared almost rudely at her, and Catherine flushed, feeling naked under his eyes.

"You seem happy enough to leave the King in the hands of my brother John and myself, having occupied yourself away from him for some time."

He was more in command now, Humphrey felt and relaxed a little, enjoying Catherine's discomfort.

She rose to her feet suddenly, startling him out of his complacency.

"Remember to whom you are speaking, my lord!" Her dark eyes flashed, and Humphrey almost leaped from his chair. "I am still the Queen, daughter of a king, and mother of a king, and now sister of a king, however much you may sneer at Charles!" She looked for a moment as if she would strike him. "Remember this; I love my son, but I promised his father that I would leave his upbringing to you and John of Bedford. However, if you try me too far, my lord, you will regret it. I promise you that!"

"I meant no wrong, Your Majesty. Forgive me for angering you. I would like you to know that I have made arrangements for the King to visit you here for a time. I hope that pleases Your Majesty?"

Until that very moment, Humphrey had thought of no such thing; but it seemed to accomplish what he'd hoped. Catherine returned to her chair, still angry, but at least prepared to talk reasonably about her son's future.

—

"I would cheerfully kill him!" Owen stood with his hands on the knife at his belt. "I wish to God I had been here when he came."

Catherine smiled up at him from the pillows.

"Just as well you were not. I've enough to do without separating two such bitter enemies as you and Humphrey have become." She waved her hand to him. "Come here, and stop behaving like a fighting cock! Your wife needs some sympathy."

He sat beside her on the bed, and took her hand. The child moved vigorously inside Catherine, and Owen laughed.

"I see we have a strong son inside there," he said, and laid his hand over the swell of her stomach, tracing the child's movements.

Catherine smiled indulgently, and drew his head down to her breast.

"You are a child yourself on occasions."

She smoothed the red gold hair away from his face, love shining in her dark eyes. His arm closed tenderly around her and their lips met in a passionate kiss.

–

From behind the shadow of some trees, Owen watched Humphrey ride through the great gates of the palace, and towards the town. As usual, he was accompanied by a group of courtiers, but that did not trouble Owen. It had been no trouble at all to bribe the groom to add a little something to the horses' fodder.

He held his horse back, keeping a fair distance behind the royal party, well content to bide his time.

From the sounds of jollity, Humphrey was well filled up with drink. No doubt this little foray was intended to provide fresh feminine company. Humphrey tired so very quickly of lady-friends these days.

Eventually, as Owen had expected, Humphrey's animal staggered under him. Very quickly, Owen drew level with the half-drunk duke.

Some of the others began to turn back, but Owen waved them on.

"It is nothing, go on ahead!"

Not recognising his voice, they obeyed and Humphrey staggered down to the ground kicking the animal in his fury.

Owen began to laugh. "I was going to beat you within an inch of your life," he said, "but now I've a much better idea." Humphrey stared at him stupidly. "Who is that? What do you want, fellow?"

Owen laughed again. "Take your clothes off, my lord duke. We'll show the people of London that you are just a man after all." Humphrey tried to run, but Owen twisted a cord around his wrists, then urged him with the point of his sword, up on to the still-dazed horse.

"You can't do this to me. I'll be the laughing stock of the whole of England." Owen turned and grimaced at the picture Humphrey presented. His fat white stomach hung over the waist of his under-drawers, and his chin wobbled freely, with no collar to restrain it.

"You need to be taught manners, my lord. I'll teach you to offend my wife."

At the edge of the town, Owen released the horse and urged it forward into the busy streets. People stopped and stared with open mouths; then someone recognised him.

"It's the good Duke Humphrey!" someone shouted.

"Who could have done such a thing?"

Owen mingled with the people to watch the horse move slowly forward, with its ludicrous burden.

"I heard it was an angry husband who did it," Owen said, to a woman standing gaping at the roadside. Immediately she began to run among her friends and Owen laughed aloud knowing that in an hour it would be all over the town.

When he was safely away from the crowds, he pulled off the dark hat that had effectively concealed his red curls.

–

Catherine had heard about Humphrey. In fact no one seemed to stop talking about the incident. But she dismissed it with a wave of her hand. For too long he had dallied with other men's wives, now apparently an irate husband had caught up with him, it was justice!

She put her hand to her aching head. She was far more worried about Joan of Arc, as everyone was calling the Maid from France. There was talk now about burning her as a witch. Catherine wondered if Charles would make any attempt to rescue the girl, but in her heart she knew that her brother had no wish to fight, even for the one person who had managed to secure for him the throne of France.

With a lift of excitement, she heard the sound of horses in the yard, and as she looked through the window, she saw the small figure of her son, Henry, cross towards the door.

He was shown into the room, and she made him a token curtsey before kissing him. He had grown a little, though his arms remained thin and bony at the wrists. His face now was sombre; almost sulky.

"What is wrong Henry? Who has displeased you?" She sat beside him, attempting to take his small hand in her own.

"You are going to have a child, Mother. They told me so, but I didn't believe it. Not with my father, the King, dead."

Catherine shook her hands in the air with exasperation. "If only people would mind their own business, and leave me to mind mine!" She turned his young face towards her. "Remember Owen Tudor? He played a great deal with you when you were little, teaching you to ride and shoot. Do you remember those things Henry?"

He nodded unwillingly, his face troubled. Catherine smiled at the memory.

"He was so good to you and will be again, Henry. We are married now and it is right and proper that I bear my husband a son. Your father, the King, was glad enough when you were born."

Slowly the frown disappeared from Henry's face. "Well, Mother, you must tell them all that you are married, and then everything will be all right."

Catherine shook her head, and moved away. "Enough trouble goes on my son, without me adding to it. Let the people of England believe that Catherine of France remains a widow. They would prefer it that way, believe me."

Henry didn't really understand, but he knew that it was not shameful for his mother to have a child so long as she was lawfully married. And he liked Owen Tudor. The big Welshmen had always been kind to him.

"Well," he said happily, "I think I would like a brother to play with me. Do you think it will be a boy, Mother?"

Catherine ruffled his fine blond hair affectionately. "I have a feeling that it will be, but we must just wait and see."

Henry came to her arms willingly now, and she was torn by pity, for his nature was so weak that it could be swayed like a straw in the wind.

"My poor son," she murmured, but Henry was happy again because all the unpleasantness was gone.

–

Catherine felt the first pain in the early hours of the morning. She shook Owen's arm, and he sat up immediately.

"Our son is going to be born today."

She turned and leaned her face against the broadness of his chest. His hands smoothed her hair from her hot forehead, and they lay silently, over-awed by the happiness that surrounded them.

When the next pain struck, Catherine cried out.

"Bring Marie," she gasped to Owen, when the agony had receded a little.

His face was white and Catherine smiled and touched his lips with her fingertips.

"It is not so bad, Owen. Please do not worry about me. I've been through this before."

The labour was brief, but difficult. When at last the cry of the newborn infant rang out fierce and strong, Catherine was almost dazed with exhaustion. She fell back as pale as a lily against the sheets.

"We have a son, Owen," she said, happiness flickering like lighted tapers in the deepness of her eyes.

He knelt beside the bed, his strong hands warm on hers. "A fine boy, Catherine. I am very proud."

She closed her eyes then, in a happy, healing sleep.

They called him Edmund. He was a happy boy from the first; and handsome, his hair red and curling like his father's.

By now, rumours of the marriage were spreading like wildfire, and many of the younger ladies were touched almost to the point of tears by the wonderful romance. Catherine was so delicate and lovely. And Owen was strong and virile. It seemed a triumph of true love over barriers of politics and protocol.

Marie doted on the child. She had become resigned to the fact that she herself was doomed never to hold a child of her own in her arms. Instead she lavished the magnitude of her maternal love on the Queen's newborn son.

"My precious little prince." She leaned over the crib, causing the nurse to raise her hands in exasperation, and softly touched the baby's cheek. "You are the sweetest boy in all the world."

There was a stir behind her, and Marie bobbed a swift curtsey as the young king came forward to peer curiously at the infant.

"He is so small," Henry smiled in wonder. "And just look at his pretty red curls."

He leaned closer, and at that moment the baby opened his eyes and waved a tiny fist in Henry's face. The young king was delighted.

"He knows that we are brothers, don't you think so, Marie?"

Marie felt tears in her throat. "I'm sure he does, Your Majesty. He is a very bright child."

Suddenly the King looked grave. "How is my mother, Marie? Is she well enough to see me, do you think?"

Marie nodded. "My lady especially asked for you to be brought to her bedside. She is well and strong, and anxious to see you." Marie longed to hug Henry, he was still a little boy for all that he was king. "Come, Your Majesty, we will go to her now."

Catherine had recovered quickly from her confinement, and leaned against the pillows, looking beautiful and rested.

"Henry, come and give your mother a kiss. I am so happy to have another splendid son. Have you seen him?"

The King went to his mother's side and held her hand in his. "Yes mother, he almost smiled at me."

Catherine encircled him with her arm.

"He will love you very much Henry; but then everyone loves you." Joyfully, she relaxed once more, still holding her son's hand. "You must promise me one thing, Henry," she added, "that you will always be kind to little Edmund."

Henry frowned earnestly. "That is an easy thing to promise, mother. I love him already."

Catherine was satisfied. Love was a powerful emotion, even in one as weak-willed as Henry, and who knew when the day might come when Edmund would depend on Henry's goodwill? She smiled fondly at her firstborn.

"You are a good son, Henry, and I'm sure that one day you will grow up to be a saintly king."

Chapter Eleven

"They have burned the Maid, then." Catherine stared solemnly at Owen, and he returned her glance with compassion. "Poor girl. And Charles did nothing at all to help her."

Catherine walked over to the window. England was lovely in the soft spring air, but she could see the leaping flames around the young French girl and the holy men, like black crows of death, standing to witness the event.

"Charles stayed in the beautiful orchards at Chinon, amusing himself with his mistress. How could he be so heartless?"

Owen moved over towards her, his hands resting comfortingly on her slender shoulders. "Don't distress yourself, Catherine, the girl had a choice and she preferred death."

Catherine turned and leaned heavily against him, her face pressed against his doublet.

"It worries me that Henry is in France at this time. He is not yet ten years of age, and yet Bedford intends to have him crowned in Paris. The time could have been better chosen, I think."

"Come Catherine, all this gloom is not good for you. Smile a little and I will play some music to lighten your spirits." Catherine turned her face towards him, regardless of the ladies' curious stares.

"Kiss me Owen. I feel strangely apprehensive, as if something dreadful is about to happen to us."

Owen held her close, his hands strong and protective.

"You are not well. You must rest more. I promise that nothing is going to happen, except that we will live a full and happy life." He bent towards Catherine, and their lips met. "Come along to the bedchamber. We will be alone, and I will comfort you."

Owen played a soft, haunting tune, and sang an accompaniment in his native Welsh, while Marie assisted Catherine into bed. Child-bearing had not spoiled the smoothness of her skin, or taken the firmness from her rounded breasts.

"You are beautiful, Catherine."

Owen stood staring down at her until Marie discreetly withdrew from the room, and then warming to the invitation in her eyes, he joined her under the sheets.

"Catherine, my lovely little wife. I can't have enough of your sweetness," he said, and kissed her smooth shoulder and the hollow of her throat.

Her hands small and sensuous caressed him. "Owen, you are so wonderful. Never take a mistress. I couldn't bear to share the joy of you with any other woman."

He buried his face in her hair. "Catherine, my wife, my queen, I could not look at any other woman when such love as yours is mine for the taking."

They moved together, like a poem with flowing liquid lines.

Outside the door of the chamber sat a young lady newly come to the court. Her cheeks flushed at the sounds issuing from the royal bedroom, but she was forced to remain where she was. She had been given an order by the senior lady-in-waiting to guard the Queen's privacy, and whatever her own personal feelings might be, she dare not disobey.

At first, young Margaret walked restlessly to and fro, trying to close her ears and mind to what was going on behind the closed doors. But then she began to think of Owen Tudor, how strong were the lines of his body and how charming his smile beneath the red-gold hair. Suddenly she wondered how it would be to have such a man make love to her. The flush on her pale cheeks became deeper, and she hung her head in case anyone should read her thoughts. But her heart continued to beat rapidly for a very long time.

–

The streets of Paris were thronged with silent crowds and Henry shuddered, looking to his Uncle John, who rode beside him for reassurance.

"Why do the French hate me so? They do not even know me."

John of Bedford eased himself into a more comfortable position in the saddle. "They have suffered a great deal of poverty, Your Majesty. Have patience; they will grow accustomed to you in time."

Henry looked down at the sullen faces of the people and doubted it. He sat up straighter. The crown was becoming increasingly heavy, making his head ache. He wished that the whole thing was over. The heat and the flies and the strangeness of the land was repugnant to him. Oh, to be back in the coolness of England once more.

He shuddered, remembering the girl who had been burnt at Rouen. He hadn't been there of course, but he had heard all about it in detail, several times over. Everybody thought that the death of the French maid was some great victory. He couldn't understand it, himself.

He wished his mother was with him. She was from France. She would know how to make the people smile and be happy. He thought longingly of the little family at home, baby Edmund in partic-ular. He always smiled so warmly, as if he really meant it. So many people had polite smiles, when really their eyes were cold and calculating.

"Will it be much longer now, Uncle John?"

He noticed the quick frown of irritation, and he knew he'd said the wrong thing again. It seemed he was always displeasing someone however hard he tried to do the exact opposite.

Then to his relief, John of Bedford smiled. "Not much longer, Henry. I know it's an ordeal, and I tend to forget how young you are."

His hand pressed the boy's shoulder, and Henry felt cheered and sat up straighter, disregarding the ache in his head.

–

Owen lay in the sweet grass, his hand shading his eyes from the glare of the sun.

Before him he could see the tiny figure of the sweet young girl who had recently joined the court. Her hair was like corn in the sun and her eyes large and sea-green. A lovely child, with tiny breasts, and the soft innocence of girlhood about her.

She was dipping before him now, her eyes lowered and a pulse beating rapidly in her white neck.

"Is there anything you require, my lord?" she said, and did not meet his gaze.

He smiled indulgently at her shyness. "I would very much like a long cooling drink."

He said it more to please her than because he really wished it, and he laughed good-naturedly as she swept quickly away to do his bidding. She was a sweet child, so pretty and untouched. It would be amusing to tease her a little.

He lay back and closed his eyes, seeing behind the lids the dark fierce eyes of Catherine, his wife, and suddenly he remembered the way in which the poor girl Jayne had been treated because he had made her with child. Hustled off into a marriage that meant exile from the gaiety of the court and before that, humiliated, made a laughing stock. He could not do that to a child so young as Lady Margaret.

"My lord, I have brought your drink."

She knelt beside him and as he opened his eyes, he met the adoration in her green ones. He took the goblet and hardly tasted the drink. The sun was striking hot against his skin and the girl was golden and lovely. She saw the desire written in his face and for a moment looked startled as if she would run; then she sank down like a golden rose beside him, docile and waiting with an eagerness that surprised both of them.

"Tonight," Owen said softly, "I will meet you here."

She nodded delicately, and a warm colour suffused her cheeks.

That evening, Catherine was especially warm and loving. She took Owen's bright head in her lap and smoothed the red–gold curls.

"I sometimes can't believe how lucky I am," she said softly, her small white teeth nibbling at his ear lobe. "It is not very common for a queen to be married to the man she loves."

Owen stretched up his hand and caressed her cheek affectionately. "I consider myself the most fortunate man on earth to possess such a wife."

Catherine bent over him. Their lips touching was like a flame. Owen turned to gain a better position and held her close, his hand inside her bodice.

"Do you still desire me, my lord?" Catherine raised her dark eyebrows questioningly.

Owen smiled. "I think it has been proved often enough, Catherine." He frowned suddenly. "I hope you still desire me."

Catherine threw back her head and a peal of laughter startled the ladies, so that they stared openly wondering what the French queen was going to do next.

"Wouldn't it be a blow to your pride, Owen, if I no longer desired you?" She bent close to him quickly. "But I do, my lord." Her meaning was clear and Owen lifted her in his arms and carried her tiny figure with ease into the bedchamber.

–

The Lady Margaret stood in the sweet grass, her tiny hands clenched to her side. Tears stood behind her long lashes and her upturned eyes were the colour of the moon.

"There must be a reason!" she said fiercely, as one by one the lighted windows of the manor-house became dark. "He would not let me wait here alone, unless there was a reason."

But he did not come; and at last, defeated, she crept back to her bed.

–

"My lady, the preparations for the move to Hatfield are almost complete."

Marie moved swiftly across the room and Catherine suddenly noticed how vivacious Marie had become since her marriage to Tom Cooper. She was slimmer and there was a radiant bloom to her skin.

"Thanks mostly to you, Marie, my ladies are all but useless when it comes to anything approaching hard work. Have you sorted out baby Edmund's clothes? So many of them are too small now."

Marie smiled joyfully. "Yes, my lady, it's all done. He's the bonniest baby I've ever seen."

Her love for the child was obvious, and Catherine was touched to the heart.

"Come here, Marie," she said softly in French. "I have news that not even my husband knows yet! I am with child once more."

"My lady," Marie's voice was anxious. "How do you feel?"

She sat at Catherine's feet, her eyes scanning the Queen's face. She looked well; her hair shone with health and her dark eyes were bright and full of humour.

"Don't worry, Marie. I have my sons with ease. Have you not noticed?" She smiled a secret smile. "My lord will be happy."

Marie stiffened. There was talk that Owen Tudor was very much interested in the pale little Lady Margaret.

"What is it, Marie? Don't you think he will be delighted by my news?"

"Of course he will, my lady. A man must enjoy being confronted with the evidence of his manhood."

There was a slight trace of longing in her voice, and Catherine was quick to notice it.

"Don't grieve; there is time for you yet," she smiled warmly. "Where is Owen? I need him with me. Please find him, Marie."

She turned to look out at the sunlit garden and didn't see the guarded expression that came to Marie's face.

"I will find him, my lady," she said softly.

-

Owen bent over Catherine's hand and kissed it almost reverently. The news Marie had imparted brought him to her side without delay.

"I am more pleased than I can tell you. How do you remain so beautiful, and yet carry my children?"

Catherine smoothed her lips against his hair. "Happiness is the answer, my lord."

She sat down carefully, and Owen leaned over her chair.

"Our baby will be born at Hatfield," she said. "I am tired of this place, and wish to be more comfortably accommodated. Do you think you will like it there?"

Owen shrugged. "Wherever you are, Catherine, that is home to me."

She reached up and pulled his head down so that their lips touched. "You will look after me always, won't you Owen?" Her eyes were misted with tears, and Owen quickly knelt before her, holding her close to him.

"You are more precious to me than life itself. I will love you and care for you so long as there is breath in my body."

She clung to him for a moment, and then with a small laugh released him.

"I must be getting old. I have become fanciful and morbid lately. I don't understand it. Maybe it will be better when we have moved into our new home."

Owen let her go reluctantly. "I shall call Marie and have her bring you some wine. You look a little pale, and it could be because of the baby. Wine warms the blood; even my mother took a little on occasion."

He smiled, thinking of his stern Welsh mother, a small but determined woman, not unlike Catherine herself.

"What are you smiling about, Owen?" Catherine said softly.

"I was wondering if we would have a daughter this time. It would be a fine thing to have a tiny replica of you; and we could call her after my mother. I would like that." Owen looked thoughtfully at the Queen's rounded figure. "You could be carrying a daughter, don't you think?"

Catherine shook her head, pushing Owen playfully away.

"I have a feeling that inside me grows another son; so save your mother's name for the next time!"

–

Hatfield was charming, surrounded by stretches of green fields, and leafy trees. Catherine walked slowly because of her size, but nevertheless enjoying her tour of the sunny, newly decorated rooms.

"I'm pleased to see you smiling, my lady."

Marie held young Edmund in her arms, ignoring the fact that he was busy chewing at the ribbon from her hat.

"I feel altogether more cheerful here. It truly seems a home at last for the Tudor family." She turned to look for her husband. "Owen, come and see the chair I have had especially made to accommodate your long frame. Do you not think it magnificent?"

Owen gently enclosed her in his arms. "This is a happy house Catherine. See how the sun penetrates into every corner."

He kissed her lovingly and neither of them saw Marie hastily make the sign of the cross to ward off any evil influences that might be made jealous by so much happiness.

Chapter Twelve

The lusty cry of a newborn infant echoed along the stone corridors, and for a moment the household held its breath. Then there was laughter and among the more devout, the mumble of prayers said in thanksgiving for the Queen's safe delivery.

Owen held his infant son, overjoyed at the strength in the small limbs of the child.

"A fine boy, Catherine."

His eyes were alight as he leaned over his wife. She was pale and exhausted against the bolster, her long hair tangled over her forehead. She smiled up at him and then closed her eyes. "Thank God," she said simply.

Owen handed the child to its nurse and sat beside Catherine, taking her hand in his.

"You must sleep now and recover some of your strength," he said, smoothing her hair away from her face tenderly.

Her eyes fluttered open. "Shall we call him Jasper? It seems a fitting name for such a vigorous boy."

A smile warmed Owen's eyes. "It shall be anything you wish, Catherine. It is an excellent name. Yes, Jasper it shall be."

She closed her eyes and sighed in contentment and relief. This son had been a long time coming, and she was not so young any more. She turned her face into the softness of the bolster and gave herself up to the feeling of drowsiness that was claiming her.

"The Queen's sons are a sight to behold!"

Marie sat in the bright sunlight, a smile of sheer contentment on her broad face. At her side was Lady Margaret, her yellow eyes shadowed in spite of the curve of her lips. Sensing something of the pain that Margaret was feeling, Marie pressed her hand. "Owen's not for you, little one; but somewhere there is a knight young and strong. And he'll come along and sweep you off your feet. You'll forget all about Owen Tudor then."

Margaret attempted a smile. She knew the older woman intended to be kind, but how could she know the depths of emotion that carried away all sense of good reason?

Marie laughed in delight. "Just look at young Edmund aim a punch at Henry. He neither knows nor cares that his brother is King of England!"

Henry too had forgotten that he was king. He rolled in the soft summer grass with his bright-haired half brothers, for once genuinely happy with no one to scold him for his lack of dignity. He dropped to his knees and tickled the fat stomach of little Jasper who promptly pulled a handful of his fine fair hair.

"Naughty boy, Jasper," Henry laughed even as he scolded and was gratified when the boy put fat arms about his neck.

"Let us hope that the young king will always be as fond of the Tudor boys as he is now."

A shadow passed momentarily over Marie's happiness and quickly she crossed herself. Margaret glanced at her in surprise. "Don't worry, the Queen will see that the children are well cared for. I should think that a good future is certain for the children of Owen Tudor."

Unaccountably, Marie did not feel reassured, but she made an effort to recapture her earlier happier frame of mind.

–

John of Bedford urged his horse forward, exhilarated by the fresh English breeze. It was so good to be home. Above him was the pale bowl of the sky, and the sun was moderate and golden: so different from the brazen sun of France.

"You are looking well, John."

Humphrey spoke pleasantly, but there was an edge of irritation underlying his words. John glanced at him, wondering at the change in his brother since he'd seen him last; then he had been young and handsome, but now his skin hung in grey folds and his breath was evil and stale.

"Humphrey, you should take more care of your own health."

"My health is all right." Humphrey's brow furrowed. "But you and our dear uncle, the Cardinal, are continually trying to thwart me."

John pursed his lips determined not to quarrel.

"You see, you do not even bother to deny it!" Humphrey's voice rose to a whine. "That

Welshman continues to flourish and breeds like a stallion on the wife of our dead brother. Why is he allowed to get away with it? Answer me!"

John's first impulse was to spur his horse forward, but he sighed and tried patiently to explain.

"Catherine is the Queen of England, mother of the King. There is no doubt that she was ill-advised in her choice of a husband; but what can we do?"

Humphrey growled low in his throat. "I'd have the heathen thrown in prison, and left to rot!" he said venomously.

"Take care, Humphrey, you are treading on dangerous ground. If the Queen had any idea of how you felt she could make life very troublesome for you!"

He looked up wryly at the peaceful sky.

"Humphrey, it is imperative that I raise money for the war. That is my main mission here."

He rode in silence for a moment, then sitting up straight looked directly at his brother.

"I'm with you on this matter, John. We must continue to fight for the French throne. It was our brother Henry's right, and it is the right of his son."

John sighed with relief. At least Humphrey was still with him on this vital issue.

The Queen was delighted to receive him. As he bent low over her hand John could not help but notice that once again she was with child. Behind her stood the tall, strikingly handsome Owen Tudor, and at her side were the two red-haired Tudor boys.

"The King will be with us in a moment." Catherine smiled warmly, her eyes clear and direct as they looked into his, and in spite of everything John was glad that she had found happiness.

"Ah, here is His Majesty now." Catherine waved her hand in the direction of the door where the courtiers were bowing before the King. "See for yourself, my lord."

John's heart turned over. For the moment it seemed as if his brother stood there before him. Then he noticed the weakness in the boy's mouth, and the slight tremble in his hands.

"Your Majesty, you have grown taller since we last saw each other in France. We had such a good time there, didn't we? The coronation was magnificent, and you acted like a true king."

Henry's face lit up. "It is good to see you again, uncle. Is the war going well?"

John felt a momentary irritation. Surely a boy of eleven, and a king at that, should take the trouble to acquaint himself with the true facts about the French campaign?

"We have our problems. I have come home in order to raise money. The army is desperately short of it at the moment." He stared thoughtfully at Henry for a moment. "Phillip of Burgundy is beginning to turn his coat, to my way of thinking. He is already demanding further concessions, and if we don't see fit to grant them, he has threatened to withdraw his allegiance."

The young king was staring with large innocent eyes, obviously worried, but quite unable to make any constructive remarks. It was Catherine who spoke.

"Phillip was always out for his own interests as you know, John. Offer him some juicy morsel, and he'll stay with England."

John sighed. "Unfortunately, we have nothing to offer. The coffers are empty."

To his surprise, Catherine laughed. "John, why must you always be so honest!" Her dark eyes twinkled as she looked at him. "Find out what he really wants, and dangle the promise of it before his eyes. His greed and natural caution will surely make him hesitate for a few months while he thinks there may be some gain for himself. That will, at least, give you breathing space."

John bowed before her, warming to her good sense. "I wish I'd thought of that myself, Madam. I am obliged to you."

Catherine rose and held her arm to him. "Come now; let us eat and drink and forget war for the time being."

Chapter Thirteen

"Don't be silly Marie. Of course I can go out!" Catherine pushed aside the bedclothes and struggled over the edge of the bed laughing at her ungainly size. "The child isn't due to be born for another two weeks, and I won't be at the abbey that long; though I admit the Cardinal makes the time hang heavy with his long speeches!"

Her eyes were sparkling merrily and she felt well and strong, the toothache that had plagued her for the past weeks having vanished into thin air.

"Let me see; now what can I wear without looking like a ship in full sail?" She padded around on bare feet while Marie exclaimed in horror at her foolishness. "Don't worry so," Catherine smiled. "The physicians have told me there is nothing better than the cold stone for relieving the cramps." She gave a little skip. "Not that I have the cramps today. In fact, I've never felt better. The red dress,

I think. Marie, hold it against me so that I can see how it looks."

She held her head to one side as she considered, and her hair long and dark, hung below her waist.

"Do I have to come?" Marie said quickly. "I find it so tiresome to sit and listen to such dour preachings."

"Nevertheless, you shall come," Catherine said gaily. "What about my husband, where is he?"

Marie looked around helplessly as if expecting him to peer out of the cupboard from among the Queen's dresses.

"Send someone to find him, otherwise he will have ridden off knowing full well that I have such a treat in store for him."

"I'll find him, my lady," Marie said softly.

–

"She knows, I tell you!" Margaret walked beside Marie, a slender, pale girl, her eyes large and luminous, almost golden in colour.

"Calm yourself, my lady. What is there to know?" Marie patted her hand affectionately. "You are imagining things, and it is foolish to show your feelings so openly."

"She knows that I love Owen Tudor," Margaret persisted. "But at the moment, she is indulgent, knowing that I am not a temptation to him."

"Why don't you allow the Queen to arrange a marriage for you? You are young and could have fine sons. Don't waste your life chasing a dream."

"Marie, you don't understand. How can I marry one man, loving another?"

Marie sighed in exasperation. "These sentiments are only going to lead to trouble. Perhaps it would be better if you left the Queen's household."

At the sharpness in Marie's voice, the girl began to weep.

"What's this? Who has dared to offend such a sweet girl?"

Marie looked up into the questioning face of Owen Tudor, with a feeling of dismay. The last thing she wanted was for him to begin taking an interest in Margaret again.

"It is only a mood, my lord," she said quickly. "The Queen sent me to find you. She would like to see you immediately. She wants company on her outing to Westminster."

As she hoped, he was distracted. "The Queen going out? Isn't that rather dangerous, Marie?"

She gave Margaret a small meaningful push, and obediently the girl quietly slipped away.

"I have told the Queen Catherine so, but as usual she refuses to listen. In fact, I have to accompany her too."

She smiled wryly at Owen and he returned her smile.

"Well, if it's what the Queen wants, then I suppose like the two bemused idiots we are, we'll go along with her!"

He took her arm, and looked down at her shrewdly.

"Did you *have* to rush the poor Lady Margaret away like that? I didn't realise that I'm such a dragon, that no young girl is safe in the vicinity!"

Marie's face was bland. "I'm sure I don't know what you mean, my lord. As for your being safe, I'm still here, am I not?"

–

The Cardinal took great pains over his appearance. The Queen was to attend today's ceremony, and that being the case the abbey was almost certain to be full. He rubbed his dry hands in anticipation. He liked nothing more than to dazzle his listeners with the eloquence of his words. He looked up with some irritation as one of his servants interrupted his pleasant line of thought.

"The Duke of Bedford to see you, my lord."

The Cardinal managed a thin smile. "Please be seated. You are welcome in my home at any time."

He more than half meant the words. He had a great respect for John's integrity, though perhaps the man was a little too noble for his own good. John sat down.

"I trust your health continues to be good?" John said sincerely enough, but the Cardinal shifted a little uneasily, remembering that it was Bedford who had successfully put a stop to the attempts that had been made on his life.

"I am well enough; but perhaps you could come to the point of your visit. The abbey, you know. I must be there very shortly."

"I need your help," John said bluntly, and the Cardinal coughed to conceal his amazement.

"What sort of help?" he asked suspiciously.

"We must have funds if we are to continue with the war. I thought you might persuade Parliament to grant me a decent allowance." He stood up abruptly, and paced around the room. "The King is your flesh and blood also; do you not think he has the divine right to rule the French throne?"

The Cardinal hesitated. It was true that he was great-uncle to the King, but money spent on food for the troops was to him money wasted! Indeed, he was beginning to think that some sort of compromise would be necessary in France. Just at the moment, however, such an opinion would be ill-favoured.

"I will speak to Parliament myself," he said magnanimously. And he *would* speak to them; instruct them to make a token payment so that no one could say help was refused. John of Bedford was popular and well respected. He must be given aid.

"I must leave now," the Cardinal said, and made a move towards the door. "But rest assured, I will do my best."

He omitted to say for whom – and smiled thinly, glad to see his nephew depart.

–

"There, my lady, we are almost ready."

Marie smiled at Catherine satisfied that the details of the Queen's dress were beyond reproach. Of course, nothing could conceal the fact that she was pregnant, but then Catherine carried her burden as if she were proud of it. Her back was straight and her small head erect as she made her way to the carriage.

The sun fell palely on the walls of the abbey, mellowing the stones and lighting the green around it. Westminster was a beautiful place, but unfortunately ceremonies bored Marie; indeed she felt herself yawning before she was even inside the doors.

"Come, Marie, courage. If I can face it, so can you!"

Catherine swept through the doors apparently oblivious to the stares of curiosity that followed her. Her dignity was unshakeable and the small ripple of gossip stopped as soon as she turned her dark eyes on the offenders.

Marie felt pride burn within her. Catherine was magnificent. She seated herself calmly beside her husband, defying anyone to utter one word of censure.

The Cardinal began to speak. He held on to his words as if afraid to part with them, and Marie had difficulty understanding him. She leaned back against the hard seat and closed her eyes.

Catherine sat up straighter, leaning a little against Owen's shoulder. The ache in her back had grown steadily, and she wished heartily that the long sermon would reach its conclusion. She glanced back at Marie and was amused to see that her head was rolling to one side, her eyes firmly closed. Lucky Marie; sleep! In fact, almost anything was better than that interminable voice going on and on. She moved again and Owen glanced down at her.

"Are you all right?" he whispered anxiously.

She nodded, though in fact, she was not at all sure she was all right. Her stomach felt hot and stretched, and there was a pain low down; it was, no doubt, due to strain, and would pass soon.

She tried to concentrate on the Cardinal's fine words, but they grew indistinct and she leaned forward trying desperately to clear the fog from her brain. The ache developed into a pain which grew and encircled her until she felt imprisoned inside a steel band. She shook Owen's arm.

"I think the baby is going to be born, soon," she said.

Frantically Owen signalled to Marie, and she took one look at the Queen and lifted her eyes to heaven.

"Hurry," Catherine said, "or the child will be born in public."

She closed her eyes feeling the fierce downward push of the baby. "Find me a couch. Anywhere, so that my child will not be born on a cold stone floor."

Marie, though pale, retained her composure. Calmly, she had sheets brought to a small side room and a large, polished wood seat was padded to make it more comfortable.

"I should have stayed at home." Catherine leaned back thankfully. "But the morning air tempted me, and I felt so well."

"That is often the way of it, my lady," Marie said, rolling up her sleeves purposefully. "But if it is God's Will that the little one be born on sanctified ground, we must make the best of it."

Catherine wanted to laugh, but the pain was engulfing her again. She could see Owen's face, anxious and white, and she bit back a scream, praying that the child would make a quick, safe entry into the world.

"Soon now, my lady. Just a little more effort, and it will all be over."

Catherine heard the words from afar and dimly saw Marie's face swim before her. What did she know about pain and suffering? Had she ever struggled, straining every muscle until it seemed the heart must burst?

But Marie continued to goad her.

"Come on, my lady, push harder. The head is almost born."

Catherine growled low in her throat with the effort. The lower part of her body burned with pain, and she felt that in a moment she would give up the struggle and succumb to the blackness that hovered invitingly around her.

There was one supreme moment of agony, and then she felt the child leave her body. She heard it cry but she felt too languid to look up. It was as if there were no bones in her body. She sighed softly, and gratefully relinquished herself to the darkness.

—

"Catherine, you *must* drink some of this; it will do you good."

Owen was leaning over her, his face drawn and his eyes dark-ringed. Catherine smiled at him, the pain now gone. She felt well again. Obediently, she drank some wine. It pierced her dry throat like a thousand needles, and brought some energy back to her. She lifted her head, and seeing the dark walls knew she was still at the abbey.

"Have I been asleep long?"

She held out her hand and brushed Owen's cheek. He smiled, a devilish light brightening his eyes.

"Several hours, Catherine. And you missed a great show. After we left the ceremony, it broke up in confusion. Each wanted to be the first to break the news that the Queen was giving birth to a child at Westminster Abbey!"

Catherine smiled. "At least we continue to entertain our people. And what of the Cardinal? Was he absolutely furious?" Owen laughed. "He refused to leave the abbey until his sermon had been completed, even though he only spoke to a handful of old men. It was a sight to behold."

"And what of our child?" Catherine asked. "I heard the cry strong and outraged. We have another son, haven't we?"

"Another strong boy. You are a true queen, Catherine. He is a handsome little man."

"I did so want a girl, Owen, a little daughter to be a companion to us both." She crossed herself quickly. "But God be praised that he is a healthy boy, like Edmund and Jasper." A sudden thought struck her. "What if we give our new son to God?" Seeing the puzzled look on her husband's face she hastened to explain. "It seems the right thing to do. Wasn't I compelled to come here today? And didn't the child come into life some weeks earlier than expected?" Tears came to her eyes. "It will be hard to leave him here, but I feel it inside me; I'm sure it is the right thing to do."

–

Marie sat in the gloom of the small bare room, holding the sleeping infant in her arms. Tears rolled along her cheeks and splashed on to the red hair that grew in profusion on the little head.

"We are to leave you behind, my little one." Her voice was thick with emotion. "And what would I give to have one such as you for my son?"

The baby stirred and thrust his pink fists into the air, pushing aside the wrappings that covered him. Marie kissed the bunched, tiny fingers, and the child opened his eyes. They were blue and clear, staring up as if the understanding of the world was in them.

"Perhaps your mother is right after all. You will be safe here, free from matters of state and politics; free from the fears of war."

The baby regarded her soberly, his eyes watchful.

She laid him down and covered him carefully. "You will be well cared for. You are still the son of a queen, even if your duty now is to God."

Chapter Fourteen

Catherine lay languidly against the pillows. The mellow afternoon sun warmed her cold hands, and rested gently and pleasantly on her face. She felt better today, she decided. The ache in her bones had almost vanished, and she didn't feel quite so tired.

From outside the window she could hear the cries of the children as they played together. She smiled, imagining Jasper running on fat, unsteady legs after his brother Edmund. And today her son, the King, would be joining them for a short rest.

Catherine moved uneasily. John of Bedford seemed anxious about the boy. He was "picky" with his food and too fond of his books. Still, he was only a child yet. There was plenty of time for manly pursuits, and perhaps some weeks in the company of Owen and the boys would be good for the King.

She looked down fondly to where Owen was lying, his bright head in her lap. Almost unconsciously, her hand ruffled his curls and he turned to her, his eyes warm and tender. "Feeling better, my love?" He kissed her fingers happily. As she nodded, she knew he had been worrying about her.

"I'm not so young any more, Owen. My middle thirties are almost here." She smiled to soften her words. "It is natural that I should be tired and listless on occasions, so don't look so dejected."

He kissed each of her fingers in turn. "You'll never be old to me, Catherine. You are even more beautiful than on the day I first saw you."

She was touched, knowing that he meant it. He didn't see how thin she'd become, how her clothes hung on her bony frame. He hadn't noticed the lines that imprinted themselves around her eyes, and on the corners of her mouth.

She felt tears rush to her eyes and wished with all her heart that she could regain some of her former vigour.

"My lady." Marie was panting in the doorway. "My lord Bedford is here, with the King." She gave up her attempt to be correct and laughed excitedly.

"His Majesty has grown so tall, I can hardly believe my eyes."

Catherine smiled. "Send them in immediately. I can't wait to see my son again."

Henry had grown. His shoulders were becoming stronger and more square, his face had lost some of its childish roundness. He came to Catherine and dutifully kissed her cheek.

"I am happy to see you again, Mother."

He hesitated, unsure of his reception. Catherine felt a pang of pity for him. He was king, and yet had nowhere to really call home.

"You are looking fine and strong, Henry," she said with more enthusiasm than truth, because his hands were still shaky and his young mouth trembled as if at any minute he would break down and cry. He brightened at her words and immediately his whole aspect changed. He sat at his mother's side as if he'd never left it, his young face filled with happiness.

John bowed to Catherine, and nodded in a friendly manner to Owen.

"I trust you are feeling well, Madam?" he said, taking Catherine's hand, and smiling into her eyes. It was obvious that he had heard about the chaos caused in Westminster some months ago when her son was born there. "I believe you are again to be congratulated? I hope you are quite recovered."

Catherine indicated that he be seated. "I have a certain listlessness at times that will not move; but other than that, I do not have cause for complaint."

She studied John carefully. He himself did not look in such robust health. He was thinner, and beneath the tan, his face was pinched and drawn. He was a man who took his responsibilities very seriously, indeed.

"What is the news from France?" she said knowing that John scarcely thought about anything else.

"Not good, Your Majesty; not good at all." He sat still for a moment, his look encompassing Owen Tudor and the young king. "We desperately need more funds. I cannot continue to fight if we are not adequately supplied with provisions; and yet no one seems prepared to listen."

His voice rose a little at the injustice of Parliament, and Catherine felt a deep pity for him. John was a good man, dedicated to his cause, but was it a lost one? She knew that Phillip of Burgundy, as soon as it was politic, would desert the English without a trace of remorse.

"What about your brother, Humphrey? Surely he is with you?" she said gently.

John grimaced. "Yes, he is with me; just so long as he doesn't have to exert himself too much. I don't know what the country is coming to."

Catherine smiled. "We shall have some refreshments; that will make you feel better. Try to forget your concerns for a while. Otherwise you will be worn out by worry." She put her hand gently over his. "I know that what you are doing is for Henry, and for your dead brother. But have some thought for your own life, John; I beg of you."

He took the wine gratefully, but even as he drank, his thick brows puckered. Catherine tried desperately to change the subject, but John was single-minded, and had not finished with the matter.

"Debts in the country amount to £164,000. Do you realise that it is three times the normal revenue!"

Catherine shook her head. "I never did have a grasp of such matters, my lord."

She caught Owen's eye, and he understood the message immediately. He rose, and smiled at the young king.

"Would you like to come into the garden, Sire? And you my lord Bedford? Try your hand at the archery range, and meet the children."

Before any protest could be raised, Owen kissed Catherine's hand. "You need your rest, my love. Shall I send Marie to help you to your chamber?"

Catherine nodded gratefully. "Yes; would you forgive me, my lord?"

John rose to his feet, and bowed. "I hope I have not tired Your Majesty?"

–

It was pleasant on the green, and John allowed himself to relax and enjoy the sun. The King strode forward and the red-haired Tudor boys rushed to greet him.

"You have fine strong sons," John said enviously to Owen. "If only Henry had lived to father more boys like this, he would have felt happier about the throne. You served with my brother, I believe," he said, suddenly feeling homesick for the good days, when the late king had imprinted his strong hand on France, and beaten her into submission.

Owen nodded. "A fine soldier. I am proud to have been one of the number with him at Agincourt."

John shook his head. "If only young Henry were a bit stronger. Sometimes I fear for the boy; he is so easily led."

Owen sighed. He loved Henry. He was Catherine's son, but he could not help agreeing with John – the boy would go any way, following the one who pulled the hardest.

"He is young yet, my lord," he said comfortingly. "It may be that he will change as he grows older."

He didn't really believe it himself, but so long as the King always had wise council, he should survive.

They stood in silence for a moment, both of them watching as the young king chose a bow and took aim. The arrow fell just short of the target, and John clapped his hands.

"Try again, Sire. Let me show you how to stand."

He hurried forward eager to help, but the King, now that it was no longer a game, lost interest and his young shoulders drooped.

"Come, Henry, show the boys how to do it," Owen coaxed softly. "You know how they copy everything you do."

Henry smiled, then, and planted a kiss on the shining faces of the two tiny boys, watching him so intently.

"Look, Edmund. And you Jasper. Sit still a moment. Watch how I aim this arrow."

With a supreme effort, he drew back the bow until it was almost pulling him off his balance; and then the arrow was flying in a true line into the target.

"Well done!"

Catherine, watching the scene from the window, was touched almost to the point of tears. She thought suddenly of her fourth son, little Owen, who would grow up to be a monk. The pain of leaving him behind was still with her, for months her breasts had ached with the milk full and plentiful; but the pain of that had been nothing to the pain in her heart.

Yet she had done God's Will. She knew that, without a shadow of a doubt. She moved from the window and climbed listlessly into bed, the slanting sun spreading warm fingers over her, and she laid her head on the warm bolster.

Hearing John talk had reminded her of home; as it used to be in the days before her marriage. The gaiety and hot sun, the laughter and happiness of the court ladies; all these things seemed to come to her mind.

And yet she hadn't forgotten her mother's spiteful tongue, and the way she had of belittling her daughter, so that Catherine felt little more than an imbecile. She shuddered. Her mother was old now and ill; her body once the most voluptuous in France was diseased and twisted. Suddenly Catherine began to cry; tears rolled down her cheeks, and silent sobs racked her thin frame.

She pulled a sheet over her head. The future had seemed so bright, and now she felt as though she were entering a dark avenue of trees, from which there would be no escape. It must be John's visit. It was his talk of war that had depressed her. She tossed and turned and finally called for Marie to come and make her comfortable.

"What is it my lady? Are you ill?" At the concern in Marie's honest face, Catherine began to cry once more.

"I feel so weak. My head aches, and my hands won't stop trembling. I am afraid."

"Oh, my lady; of what are you afraid?" She sat at the bedside and stared hard at her mistress. "Don't worry. Your blood is a little thin after childbearing," Marie smiled, relieved to have found a solution. "Your lips are pale, and see how white your hands are?" She stood up and stroked her brow thoughtfully. "Oxen liver! That will make you better. And red wine, with egg beaten into it. We'll have you well in no time, my lady."

Catherine smiled gratefully. "You always think of the practical solution. What would I do without you?" She turned her face into the softness of the bed. "I think I shall sleep now."

After only a few days eating the food that Marie prepared herself, Catherine found that her strength was returning. There was new colour in her cheeks, and all her aches seemed to vanish.

"You should be a physician, Marie. I haven't felt so well for ages!"

Owen smiled. It was good to see Catherine laugh again. He hadn't realised how much he'd missed the sparkle in her brown eyes.

"Let me take you for a drive in the coach," he said impulsively. "All too soon the winter will set in. We might as well make the most of the sun, feeble though it is."

Catherine agreed readily. The spicy smell of autumn was in the air now, and the leaves were turning into a blaze of glory.

"We must take the boys, Marie. Dress them warmly. Let them enjoy the ride with us."

Edmund rushed into the room, a thin-framed boy, quick of movement, his eyes bright and alert.

"We are going out!" he shouted excitedly, and jumped into his father's arms.

"Hey, take care; you are growing too big to rush around in such excitement." Edmund knew that the words were not a reproof. He answered by pulling gently at his father's red beard. Owen kissed him fondly, his eyes alight with pride.

"Where is your brother?"

He set Edmund down on the floor and took Jasper from Marie's arms. The baby wriggled and kicked and determinedly struggled to join Edmund.

"He has a strong will," Owen said, ruefully rubbing his forearm. "Young as he is, he will have his own way."

Side by side, the two boys were entirely different. Jasper had none of his brother's slim energy; he was broad of chest and shoulder, and stocky in the legs. The only characteristic that was common to the two of them was the bright, red gold hair that shone in the sun like a crown.

"The air is like wine," Catherine said, and she settled herself in the coach, and helped the boys into the seat beside her.

"Careful, you children; don't step all over your mother in that rude manner." Owen, even as he chided them, could not help smiling. Catherine met his eyes and in her look was all the love she felt for him. He was suddenly serious.

"Have you any regrets, Catherine?" he said, not touching her, and yet enveloping her with his love.

She shook her head. "My life would not have been worth living without you, my love."

He nodded, satisfied, and turned to look out of the window. Catherine relaxed, happy to be with the ones she loved best. She could not understand now, why she had been so melancholy. She was still quite young, and it had pleased God to give her back some of her strength.

"Look children; see the ducks swimming on the water." She leaned eagerly through the window with the boys jostling at her side.

"Slow the coach," Owen said, and lifted Jasper so that he could see.

The sound of hoofs on the road was not unduly disturbing though for a moment Catherine feared in case there were highwaymen about. Then she saw that the riders were gentlemen, resplendent in richest velvet.

"Good-day to you, Your Majesty."

For a moment she did not recognise the gross red-faced man, who was doffing his hat to her.

"What, Madam, you don't know your own brother-in-law?" He laughed, showing teeth rotten in red swollen gums.

Catherine shuddered, and attempted a smile. "Humphrey of Gloucester!" She turned quickly to look at Owen. He sat back scowling having no intention of behaving civilly. "It is a long time since we saw each other, you must agree. Your brother John visited us recently. He is well I trust?"

Humphrey's smile was unpleasant. "Not very well, I fear. He is overtaxing his strength. John always was overzealous, and of course, with us all, he grows older."

Owen's hands tensed in anger at Humphrey's insolent tone.

Catherine spoke quickly. "We must be on our way; but I hope we may meet again before too long."

Humphrey leaned forward, his evil breath penetrating into the carriage. "In the unhappy event of my brother becoming too ill to continue his duties as Regent to the King, I should naturally take over; then, Madam we should be continually in each other's company for the good of the boy." His glance swept contemptuously over the children and his cold blue eyes narrowed. "Should any accident befall young Henry, there is no question of any other offspring succeeding to the throne; you do know that Madam?"

Catherine's colour left her. "My son is well cared for as you should know, if you were fulfilling your duty as protector, my lord."

Her tone was sharp, and as Owen made to rise, she gently pushed him back.

"Drive on!" she commanded, and as the coach jolted forward, she caught sight of Humphrey smiling mockingly.

"I could kill him!" Owen could scarcely speak for anger.

Catherine lifted her hand warningly as the children stared at their father in surprise.

"What is worse, my love," she whispered, "he could kill *you*."

Chapter Fifteen

"I have come to say goodbye, Catherine."

John stood before the Queen, his face grave. At his temples were two wings of white hair; his eyes were deepset and weary.

"God go with you, and guide you." Catherine's voice broke a little. She would be truly sorry to see him leave. He was a tower of strength, a guard and protection for the young king. "Why such a sudden departure, my lord? Is there some crisis?" She waved her hand to her ladies, indicating that they bring refreshments for the lord duke.

"There is a great rising in Normandy. Many of our soldiers have been killed." He sat, obeying Catherine's silent gesture, a man grown old before his time. "And worse even than that. Phillip is wavering again. I feel sure that this time he will change sides." He put his hand to his forehead. "Without him, we would barely manage to survive."

Catherine herself held a goblet of wine towards him. "No king could ask for more loyalty than you have shown, John. Do you not think it time to come to some compromise with the French?"

John shook his head determinedly. His lips were compressed, and Catherine knew with a sinking heart that he would die rather than give an inch.

"My brother, God rest his soul, fought hard and brilliantly to secure the throne for England, as you yourself know, Madam. It is not right that I should let it all go and deprive his son of his right to rule in France."

He drank deeply of the wine and Catherine remembered in a moment of crystal clarity, the strength and courage of her first husband.

"Yes, Henry was a great man, and a military genius," she said softly.

And yet she had not loved him. He had also been arrogant and pious, and almost cold to the French bride he'd taken more as a symbol of his greatness than as a true and loving wife. Henry had been the result of their union – a weak boy even now at twelve years of age. What would his father have thought of him, had he lived?

"I'm sorry, John," Catherine smiled with an effort. "I was lost in the past. A condition afflicting only those who grow old, I believe."

John smiled. "You are still young, Madam. Your hair is as dark and glossy as it ever was. I remember when Henry first brought you home, how much I admired your hair; it seemed to glow with a life of its own."

Catherine blushed with pleasure. "A compliment always serves to bring about good humour in a lady, whatever age she might be."

"I don't know anything about compliments; when it comes down to it, I'm just a rough soldier. But I do speak the truth, Catherine, and I only wish that my brother could have lived to make the throne even stronger with more fine boys."

Catherine drew a deep breath and rested back in her seat. She had been about to tell him that she was again with child but in the circumstances, it seemed a little like rubbing salt into a wound.

Catherine watched him ride away, his shoulders straight and square. There were tears in her eyes as she turned back into the room. There was some disturbing quality about John that always made her melancholy. She drank some more of the sweet wine and tried to think of pleasant things. Her eyes grew heavy, and she slept.

She was still sleeping when Owen returned from his ride. He tiptoed towards her, and sat on the floor, his hand gently holding hers. After a while, she stirred and sighed; and then her eyes, brown and sparkling with love, were looking into his.

"Catherine don't you feel well?" he asked anxiously.

She sat up straighter, stretching her limbs. "Apart from a crick in the neck, I feel wonderful," she smiled and enfolded him in her arms. She was still warm from sleep, and he felt an overwhelming tenderness as he held her close.

"It amazes me that you give birth to such healthy, vigorous children. You are so dainty and fragile, my love." He kissed her soft cheek and then explored her mouth.

Laughing, she pushed him away. "Enough, Owen, let me wake fully from my sleep. I am in a daze." She smiled and ruffled his hair. "Play me some music so that I will be glad and cheerful. Later, I will walk a little. Marie insists that I must get the blood moving. She is full of strange ideas."

"Anything you want, Catherine," he leaned towards her and kissed her gently. "I will play until my arms ache, if it will make you happy."

–

Margaret stood just outside the door, her eyes filled with tears; it hurt her bitterly to see how much Owen Tudor loved the Queen. She twisted her hands together in an effort to control the shaking, cursing herself for being such a fool. It had done no good leaving Court for a time as Marie had suggested. She had met no gallant knight, or fine gentleman, to sweep her off her feet. But then she'd known that all along. It was Owen she loved, and she would always love him.

She moved away into the shadows. She had tortured herself enough by looking at the two of them together. He had wanted her once; would the time come when he would turn to her again?

She sighed. It was rumoured that the Queen was expecting another child. It was strange that Owen still found her attractive. She was quite old really, in spite of her tiny form and lustrous hair; now she looked ill and worn, and even that did not shake Owen's devotion.

"Lady Margaret, I am fortunate indeed to find you alone for once."

She looked up in dismay to see young Lord Kilbourn standing in her path. He had made it quite obvious for some time that he admired her, and she had tried to be cool and forbidding. Strangely enough her attitude only served to increase his interest.

"Oh, I was just going to my room. If you'll excuse me, my lord," she said, and made to pass him, but he caught her arm lightly.

"What have I ever done to make you dislike me so much?"

His lips twisted into a wry smile. Really, he was quite a handsome man, with a considerable fortune. It was such a great pity she could not love him.

"I don't understand your meaning, my lord." Margaret glanced up at him and tried to smile disarmingly.

"Margaret, I'm mad about you. Surely you must know that?" He bent towards her, his lips brushing hers.

She stood still, astonished and unable to move away. She heard footsteps behind her and to her horror, Owen's voice, soft and slightly amused.

"Is this the sort of adventure that takes place outside the Queen's chamber?"

She turned and saw the startled look in his eyes when he recognised her. His smile froze, and his eyes darted to Lord Kilbourn.

"I have asked the lady to be my wife, and if it please the Queen to give her consent, I will be happy and honoured to make the necessary arrangements as soon as possible."

Kilbourn stood tall and proud, and Margaret could not help but admire him. Just the same, she couldn't allow Owen to think that she wished for marriage.

"You speak too hastily, my lord," she said, not looking at Kilbourn. "I have not agreed, nor ever will to the marriage."

She held her head high and walked away leaving the two men staring at each other in cold anger.

-

"My back aches so much that I do not know where to put myself." Catherine looked up from the pillows into Marie's anxious face. "I wish you wouldn't worry so much; these things are natural in the process of childbearing."

She moved, trying to place herself more comfortably. In spite of her words, she heartily wished that the birth was over and done with.

"My lady, shall I bring the physician?" Marie laid a scented cloth on Catherine's face, and then placed a cushion beneath her feet.

"No, it is not time. I do not want a host of people rushing around me; they tire me more than the pain does." Catherine smiled. "I would like something to help me sleep for a few hours. I will be fresh and strong then to face the labour."

She closed her eyes and tried to shut out the dull pain that crept around her body. She should be used to it now. After all, this was her fifth child; pray to God that this time, it would be a girl. She imagined a daughter, well-made and dainty, and her heart dipped in excitement.

Marie had assured her that she was carrying in a different way this time and indeed, her stomach was high and full, with little spread on her hips.

"Here, my lady, drink this, though you look half asleep already." Marie held out the steaming herb drink and smiling, Catherine took it.

"I was just picturing myself with a daughter," she said tasting the bitter liquid, and grimacing at the shock of it. "What have you put in this, Marie?"

"Never mind about that, you just drink it up, my lady. You'll be asleep in no time."

Obediently, Catherine drained the cup. The state of the mind was very important in childbirth. A worried attitude led to more pain; her physician had told her so, and she believed him. If she could rest a while, she would tackle the ordeal with more fortitude.

She handed Marie the empty cup. "There, I have taken my medicine like a child." She smiled, and rubbed her hands over her large stomach. "The little one is resting, too. I feel no movement."

Her eyelids began to droop, and she missed the anxious look that her words brought to Marie's face.

"Stay with me while I sleep," she mumbled. "I do not wish to be alone."

Marie sat down and made herself comfortable. Soon she began to feel sleepy herself. She leaned back in the chair, and tried to put all worrying thoughts away from her.

Catherine was dreaming of red hot knives stabbing at her again and again. She screamed, and woke herself up. The pain was still there, inside her, twisting and turning like a snake.

"Owen!" she cried. "I am afraid!"

Marie, jolted out of her sleep came immediately to her side. The room seemed filled with ladies, white faces were around her, staring uncomprehendingly at their queen, writhing in agony.

"Oh, God have mercy on us!" Marie whispered, and then rounding on the distraught ladies sent them scurrying to bring the physician and the midwife and the Queen's husband.

"Owen, I cannot bear it!" Catherine moaned through clenched teeth, her thin arms wrapped around her swollen belly. Her knees were drawn up to her waist, and she rocked to and fro, trying to ease the terrible pain.

Owen hurried into the room and knelt at her side, his face ashen.

"What is wrong?" he said desperately to Marie. She shook her head in despair and began to massage the Queen's stomach in a downward motion.

The physician pushed everyone aside and examined the Queen, his face expressionless.

"The child is facing the wrong way," he said at last, "there is not much hope for either of them, I fear."

"Something must be done!" Owen said emphatically. "Marie, surely you can help the Queen?"

Marie was white and trembling. "I will try, my lord. I saw a midwife turn a child once when I was a girl in France."

Owen gripped her hand. "Please try, Marie, we have no other hope."

Marie rolled up her sleeves.

"Bring me water with salt spilled in it," she said, and the physician looked at her in astonishment. When the bowl was brought, she plunged her arm into the water right up to the elbow.

Without drying it she went to Catherine and gently began to probe. There was silence in the room except for the faint moans that came from the Queen's white lips. Beads of sweat stood out on Marie's face, and Owen carefully wiped them away.

"I think I am succeeding," Marie said, hope lighting her eyes.

Soon Catherine began to stir; the walls of her womb began to contract, and within a few minutes the child was pushed into the world.

"It is witchcraft," one of the ladies murmured, and hastily crossed herself.

The physician stepped forward and attended the Queen. "She is very weak," he said, "but she will live." He turned to Marie who was wrapping the baby in a square of linen. "You are truly skilful; and the Queen owes you her life."

Catherine opened her eyes and saw the faces around her, curious and staring.

"My baby," she said faintly, "I wish to see my baby." Owen went close to her, his hand caressing her face. "You must sleep, my love. This has been a terrible ordeal for you. You shall see the baby later, I promise you."

Weakly, Catherine closed her eyes. She could not fight the darkness that was engulfing her. She sighed, and at least there was no more pain.

–

When Catherine opened her eyes, she found the sun dazzling her and somewhere, quite near was the sound of sobbing. She felt cold. Her hands and feet were lifeless, and when she tried to move it was as if she had turned to stone.

"Owen," she said softly, and immediately he moved into her line of vision, his hair shining red like a halo.

"Catherine, my dear wife!" He bent towards her, his cheek hot against hers. The crying had stopped abruptly as if muffled by a hand. She tried to turn her head but the effort was too much.

"Where is Marie? I must thank her." The words were thin, without body or resonance, and she scarcely recognised her own voice.

Owen made a gesture, and Marie appeared at his side. Her eyes were swollen and red though she attempted a smile.

"You gave us a scare then, my lady, and no mistake." She adjusted the sheets as though to gain time. "You are regaining your strength slowly, and if you eat some of my good broth you will feel much better."

Catherine nodded. The hot liquid warmed her, and soon the feeling began to return to her legs.

Marie beamed as she spooned out the last of the broth. "There, that will make you well." She set down the bowl and began to bathe Catherine's face in sweet scented water. "It will freshen you, my lady."

Catherine suffered her ministrations in silence, and when she was finished she turned to Owen.

"Our child. You promised me I could see him."

Owen closed his eyes for a moment and then sat at the edge of the bed, taking Catherine's cold hand in his own.

"It was a girl. I called her Margaret after my mother; I knew you would wish that."

Something in his attitude struck a chill into Catherine's heart. "My baby. My little girl. Where is she?"

Owen could not speak. He covered his face with his hands and his broad shoulders began to shake.

"Marie, bring me my daughter." Catherine's voice was stronger now. "Is she deformed or ugly? What is wrong with her?"

Marie hesitated, and then went to the crib in the corner of the room, lifting the tiny bundle, and carrying it carefully to Catherine.

The child was perfect. Her features delicate and beautiful, her hair dark and glossy. And she was dead.

Tears poured from Catherine's dark eyes and fell like diamonds in the child's dark hair. Owen rose and took the baby gently away.

"It is the will of God, Catherine," he said quietly. "We must try to accept."

She looked up at him as if he was a stranger. "I will never accept. I will always grieve for my own little girl who had no chance to live."

Her voice was cold and empty and she watched with wide eyes as Marie took the infant from the room.

"Catherine, you might have died, too."

Owen sat close to her and tried to comfort her. She was listless and apathetic, her face empty of all emotion. She turned her face away from him and closed her eyes; and for the first time in their marriage, Owen felt that his wife did not want or need his presence.

Chapter Sixteen

The ground was hard beneath the horse's hooves, and Owen delighted in the wind and rain that beat against his face. At his side rode Lady Margaret, the hood of her cloak blown back from her face, and her yellow hair streaming in wet curls behind her.

"Are you sorry now that you decided to come with me?" he shouted.

The wind took his words and dispersed them, and he laughed at the bewilderment in her face. Through the trees, he saw a hut and held up his hand for Margaret to stop. He helped her down and pushed open the door. It was bleak and dusty inside, but at least it was shelter until the rain stopped.

Margaret shrugged out of her dripping cloak and laughed up at him, her face shining and flushed, her hair in tendrils that clung like a baby's to her skin.

His heart turned over as he compared her to Catherine. It was six months now since the death of the baby and yet the Queen still remained pale and listless, her hands lying like dead leaves against her black dress. Every time he looked into her eyes, he saw a reproach there, as if she blamed him for the tragedy. That's why he was here with Margaret now; he needed to get away from the cloying atmosphere of the Queen's chamber.

"It is foolish of us to attempt to ride in this, my lord." She smiled, her teeth white and strong in her young face, the colour whipped into her cheeks by the wind only making her more attractive.

"I have enjoyed it thoroughly," he said, sitting down on the rough bench against the wall.

She sat beside him, suddenly quiet, her eyes shy and deep as they looked into his.

Owen reached out and took her hand. "I am very grateful to you, Margaret. I want you to know that."

She curled her fingers around his and stared at him, her breath almost leaving her.

"I do not need gratitude," she whispered.

For a moment he hesitated. He loved Catherine even though she seemed to care nothing for him now, and it was never his intention to be unfaithful.

Her eyes were clear and wide and warm like honey, as they looked into his. She swayed towards him and he felt the fullness of her breast against his.

Desire swept into his body like a fire. Margaret was young and healthy; a beautiful girl. He put his arm around her – even in the heat of the moment, comparing her firm flesh to the delicate thinness of his wife.

Margaret gasped, and thrust herself towards him, her hands reaching for his face to draw it to her. She was eager and energetic, and Owen felt warm and needed, flattered by her passion for him.

His hand expertly unfastened her bodice, and she did not withdraw. Her skin was pink and golden and excitingly different to Catherine's brownness. Passion sang in his blood, and in his head driving out all thoughts but the immediacy of his desire.

They rode back home in silence, Owen relaxed and happy; a man again. At his side, Margaret's face was flushed with joy; her eyes shone as if the sun was trapped within them.

From her herb garden, Marie watched their approach. Her face was troubled. She guessed at once that they were lovers, and she could not find it in her heart to blame Owen. The Queen had spurned his affections for too long.

Poor Catherine. She may never recover from the death of her baby girl. She walked about like a dead thing herself with no smile touching her lips even when her sons sat with her.

Marie crossed herself. Please God that the Queen would return to her full senses before long. She thought of Catherine's father; so mad that he didn't care even if he dressed himself. Perhaps the Queen had inherited the weakness, and would become as he was. But no. Catherine's sickness was a temporary thing, brought on by grief; the best thing would be for Owen to make her with child again.

Marie placed her hand on her own stomach; even now after five months she couldn't believe that she was with child. The baby moved as if feeling the warmth of her hand. Marie whispered a prayer that all would be well. Tom was almost beside himself with joy. He had thought himself too old to be a father now.

She turned her back on the couple riding towards her to save the embarrassment of being seen, and stooped down to tend to her plants.

Catherine was saying her prayers when she heard the sound of horses outside. She did not lift her head to look or take her mind from her occupation, but one of her ladies exclaimed and made a sudden, startled movement, and Catherine was distracted.

She knew, with just one look, and her heart turned to stone within her. How could he be so cruel and faithless? He was hers; he belonged to the Queen of England. How dare he outrage her in this manner?

Her ladies stood motionless, waiting for her to move. She looked down again and resumed her prayers; but her heart was heavy, and for the first time in months she felt tears warm and fast fall on to the crucifix in her hand.

–

"I will always love the smell of the forest."

Margaret lay on her back in the deep coarse grass, her pale arms stretched above her head. Owen looked down at her with affection, admiring the fullness of her breasts beneath the soft, smooth velvet of her dress.

"You are looking exceptionally lovely today, little yellow flower."

He bent over and kissed her soft lips, but somehow there was no excitement, no warming of the blood. Today he had seen Catherine, dark as a raven in her crimson gown; and now Margaret seemed insipid by comparison.

It was strange, but he felt that his wife had been flirting with him. Her brilliant eyes had looked provocatively into his, and when he had stooped to kiss her dutifully on the cheek, she had turned her mouth to him in a sharp, stirring kiss. He could feel it now; the way her little tongue probed his and her small white, almost feline teeth, had been sharp against his lips.

"Come back to me!" Margaret complained. "You are far, far away. I don't like to be shut out from your thoughts." She wound her arms around him and pulled him close. "Do you not wish to love me a little, Owen?"

She nuzzled against him; every part of her was soft and with a fullness that had now lost its savour. He longed for Catherine's fineness, the fragile bones that felt as if they would break beneath his caress.

He tried to move away, but Margaret held him close; her hands busy and her lips clinging to his.

She was like a whirlpool that sucked in victims giving them no avenue of escape. Suddenly he was inexplicably angry. He pressed down against her, heedless of her sharp cry of pain using her in blind animal fury, until at last he fell back into the grass and stared sightlessly up at the sky.

–

They rode back home without either of them speaking a word. Margaret sobbed ceaselessly, the tears slipping large and plentiful down her cheeks. She knew it was over, finished; his love was dead and nothing would resurrect it. She sought in her mind for a way out of her dilemma. She was with child, and she could hardly remain as one of the Queen's ladies now.

At the gateway, she dried her eyes, and held her head high. Owen turned to her, his eyes pleading for understanding.

"I can give you a dowry," he said. "It will help you to make a good match." She nodded her head, and then rode away from him without speaking.

It took a while, but soon she had erased the marks of the tears from her face, and in fact, her eyes looked more luminous and yellow than ever.

"Tell Lord Kilbourn I will see him," she said to her servant, her heart beating quickly. What if he didn't want to associate with her now? But then he was at the door, a sardonic smile on his face.

"Please enter, my lord." Margaret's voice trembled and from the lift of his eyebrows she knew he was aware of her nervousness. He came and stood before her, and she was disappointed by the smallness of his stature in comparison to that of Owen Tudor.

"I am at your service, my lady," Lord Kilbourn said softly, a curious inflection to his voice.

Margaret coughed; she found it difficult to begin.

"I believe that you wished to marry me, my lord?" she said at last, her eyes downcast and her hands twisted together.

"You speak as if I no longer wish such a thing," he said, and his hand, strong, almost cruel, forced her chin up so that she had to look into his eyes.

"Do you?" she said fearfully, trying desperately to free herself.

Instead of answering he drew her into the bedchamber and without ceremony pushed her back against the covers.

"My lord, what is the meaning of this?"

"I feel I have the right to inspect the goods before buying," he smiled cruelly, and tugged so hard at her bodice that it came away in his hands. She lay there, her eyes closed against the humiliation.

"Not bad for a woman they call the Tudor whore," he said, "and what is good enough for the husband of the Queen shall be good enough for me; especially with the handsome sum of money I have been offered by Owen Tudor."

Long after he had left, Margaret sat at the window and stared out at the green grass and the tall trees pointing to the scarlet-streaked sky. She would make the best of her marriage to Lord Kilbourn; who knew but that he might mellow with time and in a strange way, there was something exciting about his very cruelty to her. As she glanced down at her torn bodice, a flush of anticipation coloured her cheeks.

—

"Come along, Edmund, hit Jasper back. He must not be allowed to get away with such antics!" Owen fell laughing on the green watching his sons wrestle with each other.

"See how strong Jasper is, Uncle Owen?" Henry stood proudly, watching his half-brothers, with fist clenched as if he would have liked to join in the mock battle.

"Aye, he's a sturdy lad; but then Edmund is quick and wiry and escapes most of the blows. Go on, see how you fare against them."

The young king went hesitantly forward, but the two Tudor boys quickly swooped on him, and soon he was laughing and tumbling, happy to forget that he was ruler of England.

"I see our sons are having a fine time," Catherine smiled serenely, and as Owen quickly got to his feet, she rested her small hand on the sleeve of his doublet. "Would you care to walk a short way with me, my lord?" Her eyes were dark and mysterious as they looked into his. Owen felt his blood stir.

The grass was soft and lush beneath their feet and the cold breeze ruffled Catherine's hair so that strands of it drifted free and rested tantalisingly against his face. The scent of it reminded him vividly of moments of extreme intimacy, and he longed to hold her and make her truly his wife again.

"You are looking very well, Madam." His tone was formal and the words were not the ones he wished to speak.

Catherine smiled at him amused. "Yes, I feel much improved, both in spirits and in body; thanks mainly to the administrations of the faithful Marie. Would you believe that she brings me leaves from the fields to eat?"

She laughed and Owen smiled warmly at her good humour.

"She is remarkable. We both owe her a great deal," he said, wondering why on earth he wasn't telling his wife that she had captivated him with her beauty, and that he wanted nothing more under the sun than to love her.

"Soon she will have her child," Catherine said, glancing up at him mischievously. "I envy her, my lord."

Owen felt his mouth go dry. "Catherine, just allow me to…" He got no further; the Queen lifted her hand, and darted away from him.

"My son, I do believe he is injured!"

He followed her across the grass to where Henry was sitting, his hand held to his eye. At his side stood Jasper, his tiny fists clenched and his lip pushed forward as if he would weep any moment.

"Don't scold him Mother," Henry said bravely trying to smile, though by now his eye was quickly darkening into a bruise. "It was an unfortunate accident, it really was."

Catherine scooped Jasper into her arms. "That is treason," she said playfully. "A vicious attack on your king. Shame on you Jasper Tudor!"

The boy began to cry and immediately Henry held out his arms.

"Don't tease him, Mother, it doesn't matter at all. See, it has almost gone now."

Jasper went to him and patted his cheek with more affection than gentleness, and Henry winced. "You are a tough little fighter; one day you will be a great general in my army."

Edmund was not to be outdone. "I want to be in your army too. I will fight as good as Jasper, you'll see!"

"All right, both of you shall be in my army."

Henry smiled, pleased to have made the boys happy; and Owen wondered if Henry would still remember his promise in years to come.

"Come, the children are satisfied now." Catherine took his arm once more, and led him towards the palace. "I have had enough of the sunshine, and the breeze is growing quite cold. Will you accompany me to my chamber, Owen?"

She slanted her eyes at him in a way that spoke her thoughts quite clearly. He put his arm around her waist and she fitted against him as if she was made for him. He felt a flush rise to his cheeks. It was almost like being a boy again and in love for the first time.

Slowly he bent and kissed the top of Catherine's silky hair.

Chapter Seventeen

Catherine was like a girl again. She laughed and danced as if she had never known a moment's illness in her life. Owen attended her as if afraid she would disappear into a mist, and the courtiers talked behind their hands at the openness of the couple's love for each other.

"I don't give a fig for anything the gossips say." Catherine lay on the bed, her hair spread around her like a dark cloak. "I have been the subject of Court gossip for many years, and it hasn't been allowed to interfere with my life. I live it the way I please."

Marie, her round face flushed, brought Catherine a bowl of orange water. "We all know that, my lady," she said wryly.

Catherine glanced at her. "You are incredibly large, Marie. Surely the child will be born soon?"

No longer did the thought of Marie's baby have any sting. Catherine herself was with child again.

"I don't think I could carry it much longer, my lady." Marie sat heavily in a chair. "I already feel like a cow about to calf."

Catherine laughed good–humouredly. In all truth that was an accurate description of how Marie appeared.

"At least you will be sure of a big healthy child," Catherine said comfortingly. She rose from the bed. "I must dress, and join my lord."

She chose the red dress that Owen loved so much. It was still snug over her flat stomach; but soon, the seams would be let out to accommodate her as she grew with her pregnancy.

"Catherine, are you nearly ready?" Owen entered the chamber like a breath of fresh spring air; his face rosy from the vigorous ride he had enjoyed, and his eyes shone blue and bright.

"I am ready, my lord, except for my hair." Catherine ran her slim fingers through the dark glossy strands voluptuously. "Would you care to comb it for me, Owen?"

He came and stood behind her, his hands caressing and tender. He lifted her hair, and kissed the nape of her neck.

"Come on you two, you will never get out at this rate!" Marie ushered them away as if they were children; and laughing, hand in hand they left the chamber.

Once she was alone, Marie quickly cleared away the Queen's toilet articles, and then went to her own quarters. It was good to rest and be away from the prying eyes and gossiping tongues of the court ladies.

The ache in her back was unpleasant, but not desperately so; perhaps some leaf tea would help a little. As she rose there was a strange sensation, low in her stomach. She gasped, her baby was about to be born!

She quickly lay down again and loosened her clothing, trying to fight the panic that was rising inside her. Perhaps Tom would come and find her. Or Catherine send for her services. But the child was impatient, this was no time for hysterics. Marie drew up her knees and stoically pushed her bawling healthy son into the world. And in this the greatest moment of her life, she was alone.

–

The small room gleamed in the cheerful firelight, filled with the homely smells of clean linen and fresh baking. In the bed, in the centre of the room, lay Marie, her newborn infant in her arms. At her side was Tom, his face illuminated with happiness and filled with honour because next to his wife sat the Queen of England, with her husband and children at her side.

"How on earth did you manage it all alone?"

Catherine stared at Marie in genuine concern, her slim hand resting lightly near the baby as if longing to touch him.

"There was no choice my lady. And in any case, the birth was an easy one. Over in a few minutes."

Catherine shook her head. "I envy you. I pray my own will be as good. I have had enough of difficult confinements!"

She smiled up at Owen as if to assure him that he was not to blame in any way, but that the fault, if any, rested in her own self.

He touched her cheek softly, his eyes tender. "I hope this time, Catherine, you will have the daughter you've longed for."

She nodded. "I will. I feel it inside me." She rested her hands protectively over her skirt, as if she could really feel the child. "She will be pretty and healthy, a joy of a girl." She smiled suddenly at Marie. "But this is your day, and you have borne a good strong boy for your husband, just as a good wife should." She turned again to Owen. "We must see that there is an endowment arranged for him. I owe that much, at least, to Marie."

The baby began to cry, loud piercing sounds of anger. He doubled up his fists and his small face reddened.

"He cares nothing for endowments!" Owen laughed. "The little boy wants to be fed."

Catherine rose and took the hands of her sons. "We will leave you now. Rest and get well quickly, Marie. I shall be lost without you."

-

The days passed peacefully for Catherine. She felt well and happy, and as her pregnancy advanced, her feelings of melancholy left her altogether. She laughed a great deal and played constantly with Marie's baby, who was a cheerful boy, very much like his mother in appearance.

"It is good to see you this way, my lady." Marie sat sewing more royal baby clothes for the new girl child.

"You seem as you were before…" She stopped speaking and looked at her mistress in confusion.

But Catherine merely smiled. "Don't be afraid to speak of the death of my baby girl, Marie." The Queen's eyes were clear and untroubled. "God chose to take one child from me, but I am to have another, so He is good to me."

Marie sighed with relief; the Queen was indeed well again. Her cheeks had filled out and there was a healthy sparkle to her dark eyes. If only her child was a strong healthy girl, everything would be wonderful.

"Jacina," Catherine said suddenly, "isn't that a pretty name?" She smiled and stared out of the window across the green fields. "Yes, I think Owen will like that very well."

—

The marriage was arranged so quickly that Margaret scarcely had time to think. It was not what she wanted her wedding to be like at all, but speed was necessary before her condition became too obvious.

A few days after the wedding, Lord Kilbourn hurried into her apartment, his face filled with an almost malicious humour. She shuddered, and drew her wrap more closely around her shoulders.

"What is it my lord?" She made way for him to sit beside her and was surprised when he took her hand in his.

"My dear Margaret, I've heard some news. Queen Catherine is with child once more."

Margaret felt a momentary pain inside her. So Owen had transferred his affections once more to the Queen, and with very little delay.

Lord Kilbourn got to his feet, and stood before her. "The Queen will have sympathy with a woman in the same condition as herself; and by the same man too! It really is quite amusing."

Margaret looked down at her hands. "I couldn't; the Queen hasn't been well. The shock, it could do her harm."

Kilbourn waved his hand impatiently. "That is for Owen Tudor to worry about." Margaret looked at him in bewilderment. "Why are you doing this? You don't need the money. Is it revenge?"

Her husband smiled. "Let us say, I like to see justice done." He caught her arm tightly. "You will see him tonight. I will arrange it." He bent forward and kissed her lips. "I will give the little Welsh brat my name, but Owen Tudor will pay dearly for the honour I do him."

–

"My lady Margaret, it is good to see you looking so well and as beautiful as ever." Owen bent over her hand. "It was very kind of you to invite me to your home. I am happy to see how comfortable you are as Kilbourn's wife."

She gestured for him to sit down. "I will send for refreshments, and then perhaps we may talk, my lord?"

There was a thickness in Margaret's throat. She felt her hands shake and wondered how she could ever make herself ask Owen for more money. She closed her eyes in anguish.

At last, when he was drinking the wine and staring at her with his eyebrows raised, she knew that the moment could be put off no longer. She looked deep into her cup, anywhere but at him.

"My husband has instructed me to ask about the child's future, my lord." She glanced at him quickly and then lowered her lashes once more so that he couldn't see the expression in her eyes.

"I don't understand you, Margaret. I made an ample allotment of money on you at your marriage."

"I don't know anything about it, my lord," she said, softly apologetic in spite of herself.

"It was very generous, I assure you. I am very grateful to you, and in your debt."

His tenderness and courtesy brought tears to Margaret's eyes.

"It's not for me, my lord. I would rather go away and forget all about it, but my lord Kilbourn, he feels…"

The door opened suddenly, and it was obvious that Lord Kilbourn had been listening outside.

"I feel that it is not enough, my lord." His tone was almost insolent and Margaret saw Owen stiffen. She knew that softness would gain what threats would not.

"The child, my lord," she said quickly, "will need an income so that when the time comes he can set up in a home himself." She put her hand on his arm. "Please Owen, for the child." She saw him waver and then Lord Kilbourn strode across the room.

"There are other things to take into consideration now, my lord." He smiled unpleasantly.

Owen looked at him in bewilderment. "What other things? Speak your mind! I don't like riddles."

Lord Kilbourn didn't answer immediately; he looked across at his wife, and then stared insolently at Owen.

"I hear the Queen is to have a happy event quite soon; isn't it a coincidence?"

Owen flushed red with anger. He picked up his hat and strode to the door.

"Threats will not make me hand over any more money to you. The Queen knows about Margaret, so you are wasting your time. Good-day to you, my lady."

Margaret stood in stony silence, listening to the dying hooves outside. She knew that her husband would not be bested. He would tell the Queen now, even if there were no gain in it for himself. If only he had left matters in her hands; she could have won Owen around, she knew it. She glanced across at Lord Kilbourn, and to her astonishment he was laughing!

"This is what you wanted all along," she said in fury, "it wasn't the money; you wanted to see him humiliated. Well, he was more of a gentleman than you'll ever be!"

He struck her sharply across the face. She stared at him in cold dignity, and he struck her again; then suddenly he took her in his arms.

"If blows won't melt you, I know something that will."

He picked her up and carried her into the bedchamber and even as she despised herself and him, she felt excitement rise and flow like wine through her veins.

–

Cardinal Beaufort rubbed his hands together in an expression of what could almost be called glee. His old enemy was at the door, and there was little doubt that he had come to ask some favour.

"Show Duke Humphrey in, and then bring some wine," he ordered his servant, and seated himself in his tall backed chair, his hands folded, his features composed.

Humphrey bowed briefly and then sat hands on knees facing his uncle. His cheeks were flushed, though whether from drink or exertion it was hard to tell.

"Is there something I can do for you, my lord Duke?"

The Cardinal spoke quietly intoning the words as if conducting a service. He had observed the way Humphrey's hands trembled and was pleased to see that a great deal of the man's force and personality had deserted him. It was indeed a long time since he had dared to attack the person of himself, Henry Beaufort, but he would never be allowed to forget it, not for one moment.

"My brother John is ill. It is feared he will not recover," Humphrey said bluntly, well aware of the Cardinal's hate; but he needed him now. He had strength and position and most of all, great wealth. "In which case, my lord as you must realise, I will be Regent to the King; he is still very young and needs a firm hand to guide him."

The Cardinal narrowed his eyes, and lifted the cup to his dry lips. Humphrey, as Regent, was an entirely different prospect to Humphrey, the younger duke, squandering his health on women and wine.

"Pray continue," the Cardinal said, cautiously. "You have my full attention."

"I suggest we combine our forces on this issue, and settle once and for all our policy in France," Humphrey said briskly. "You know as well as I how much money can be made from war."

The Cardinal lifted thin eyebrows. Bold statements were likely to be misconstrued if overheard by the wrong people.

"I'm not sure I quite follow, but please do not allow me to distract you from your line of thought." He poured more wine, and Humphrey immediately drank deeply.

The Cardinal allowed himself a small smile of satisfaction. Give this one a little more time and he would surely make an end to himself with over-indulgence.

"We must send money and provisions, in order that the war may continue." Humphrey's eyes seemed to protrude with the urgency of his feelings. "We cannot allow the French to become too strong, or they will endanger us all."

The Cardinal put down his drink and arched his fingers, tip to tip. He liked the gesture. It appeared to indicate that he was deep in thought, when really he was playing his favourite game of cat and mouse.

"Personally, I feel the time has come to compromise," he said at last, and his eyes were sharp as needles, as they rested on Humphrey's face. His nephew stared back at him uncomprehendingly for a moment; then it dawned on him that the Cardinal was refusing his help.

"But it is as much in your own interests as mine," Humphrey said, falteringly. "How can you refuse? The King is your own flesh and blood!"

The Cardinal rose, indicating that the meeting was at an end. Humphrey leapt up from his chair in a fury.

"The people of England will not like your attitude my lord." He was a gross man, dissipated by excess, but now in his righteous indignation he almost had a sort of dignity.

"When the people find they have food in their bellies they will thank me on bended knees," the Cardinal smiled unpleasantly. "My servant will show you out."

Humphrey strode to the door.

"I should have killed you years ago. You do not care for the people, only for yourself!"

He staggered suddenly, and slowly toppled to the ground, clutching his chest. For a moment Henry Beaufort was tempted to leave him there to die, like a dog; but then he remembered he was a cardinal, and it would not look right if Humphrey should die while within his walls; their enmity was too well known.

"Bring a physician," Cardinal Beaufort called to his servant. "Duke Humphrey has been overcome by the heat; and perhaps a little too much wine." He held his hand up as the servant turned to go. "Wait, it may be better to take the Duke to his home, and leave it to the members of his own household to see to his well-being. I'm sure he will be quite recovered in a few hours."

Chapter Eighteen

"How are you feeling now, Humphrey? Very much improved, I trust?"

Catherine sat beside the bed, appalled at the change that had come over the Duke since the last time they met. He was propped against the pillows, his face sunken, and with a frightening bluish tinge to his lips. She was pleased now that she had overcome her disinclination to make the journey at all.

"I am well enough, Madam, but none the better for seeing you. And in such a state!"

He pursed his lips like a truculent boy, and in spite of her anger at his rudeness, Catherine could not help but feel indulgent towards him. He obviously was so used to giving the women of his household the sharp end of his tongue, that he had forgotten to whom he was speaking.

"Gently, my lord Duke," she said severely. "I will ignore that remark. Now, I understand you were taken ill at the home of the Cardinal. Is that not so?"

She could not help smiling. No doubt the dried up little churchman had been in a fine dilemma, having his bitterest enemy at his mercy.

"You have spies everywhere, I see. So there is not much point in my denying it." Humphrey slumped back petulantly.

Catherine rose. "I have come at a bad moment, my lord. Perhaps you are in pain, and conversation is difficult for you?"

He turned and hoisted himself up with an effort.

"Yes, I have a pain, Your Majesty," he said fiercely. "I have a hurt that is nothing to do with my illness." He stared at her swollen figure vindictively. "My brother John of Bedford is stricken, and lies near to death in France. I lie here helpless; and you, who are mother to the King, breeds bastards by that Welshman!"

The veins in his temples stood out, and Catherine thought he would drop back into a fit at any moment.

"How could you allow him near you after my brother was your husband? You were married to the King of England and France, Madam, and yet you let that pig into your bed."

"Enough!"

The word was spoken low and yet it silenced Humphrey's tirade. He sank back and stared glassily at her.

Catherine stared at him, her eyes glittering darkly. "If you ever speak to me that way again, I will kill you myself," she said, with such conviction that Humphrey could not fail to believe her.

"And I will kill the Welshman one day, Madam; with every bit of my strength I will hound him. He is only safe while he shelters behind your skirts."

Catherine stepped forward, and struck Humphrey across the face.

"It would pay to remember that I am still the Queen of England. Once the King is out of tutelage, where will be your power then?" Her eyes sparkled with triumph. "Be afraid Humphrey, it would be wise of you."

She turned and left him, her heart thumping painfully. She had never before wished for the death of anyone, but now she prayed that the Duke would be carried away by another attack; and then she would know that Owen and their sons were safe. Shaking, she climbed into her carriage.

"Take me home quickly," she said, and sank back wearily against the seat.

It was several days before Catherine regained her serenity of mind. The man was ill, obviously demented; the best thing by far was to ignore his threats. What could he do? Make an attempt on Owen's life? She smiled with pride. He would have to be up very early in the morning to catch Owen unawares.

"Come along, my lady, have some of my special broth." Marie was at her side, anxiously fussing over her. "You must think of your baby, that lovely daughter you mean to have. Eat now, and forget anything that disturbs you."

Marie was well and strong, and her son was growing into a fine handsome boy, with black curly hair. She took him everywhere, setting him down always close at hand, so that she could continually keep an eye on him. He was very content and never seemed to cry, and to Marie, he was the sun and moon rolled into one.

"Marie, will you make me a promise?" Catherine smiled as Marie nodded eagerly. "You do not know what I ask yet."

"Anything that will make you happy! I will promise it, my lady," Marie said.

"I want you to promise to look after the children, should anything happen to me." She raised her hand as Marie made to protest. "I'm not being silly and fanciful. I just want to know that you will care about my children."

There were tears in Marie's eyes. "I do care, my lady, haven't I helped bring them up? I would guard them with my life."

Then Catherine nodded. "Good, that is what I wanted to hear. Now no more morbid talk. Bring out the needlework, and we will see how my Jacina's clothes are coming along."

–

The coach bowled along at a brisk pace, and Margaret shivered inside even though the air was warm. She glanced from under her eyelids at her husband. He was quite relaxed, with no flicker of doubt or hesitation on his clean-cut features.

"My lord," Margaret ventured, but he waved her to silence and she subsided, a fluttering feeling inside her, making her almost sick.

He was wrong, she felt it in her bones; he would come out of this the worse. Tears welled into her eyes. She tried to brush them aside without him noticing, but Lord Kilbourn missed nothing.

"Crying will bring you nothing but a red face, and that only serves to make a woman plain," he said, not unkindly.

"The Queen has a terrible temper," she blurted out. "She will not listen favourably to us, I know it."

"Hush, Margaret, you don't know what you are saying. In any case, if Owen Tudor sees us coming, there is no doubt he will stop us from entering, and will be ready to agree to our terms."

He looked ahead of him, his expression bland.

"I have no terms of my own; they are all yours, my lord," Margaret spoke stiffly.

She was still angry with him, but he took no notice of her. She was too puny to have any effect on him. He would do just what he had decided.

—

"Oh, I feel good today." Catherine stretched her legs and pushed the sheets away from her. "See how the sun shines. It is a good omen; this is the day the midwife says my child will be born." She turned to Owen and ruffled his silken red hair. "Wake up, my lord. How can you sleep on a day such as this? Don't you know the day is half gone, and we still lie in bed?"

Owen drew her to him and smoothed back her hair. "Let us pretend it is still night." He bit her ear sharply, and Catherine squealed. "Owen! Enough of your nonsense; look here are the children to see us."

Edmund and Jasper climbed on to the bed, and Catherine immediately slipped from under the sheets.

"To stay in there with you three Tudor fiends is asking for injury of some sort or another," she laughed. "Go on, boys; tell your father it is time he was out of bed."

She called her ladies, and they helped her to dress, against a background of screams and shouts from the children, as they fought with their father.

"Shall I take the children away, my lady?" Marie looked anxiously at Catherine, but she waved her hands and smiled. "Don't worry, I'm feeling fine today; see how the sun warms the room and turns the hair of my three loved ones into beaten gold?"

She sat and watched them, a smile on her lips, her hands resting on her full stomach. Soon her daughter would be born, her little Jacina. It might even be today. She felt a lift of excitement, tinged with fear. Please God, let the birth be a good one; and the baby be well and strong.

At last, Owen emerged from the rumpled bed, a son on each arm. "Madam, do these belong to you?" He pretended to drop the boys, and they yelled in an ecstasy of fear. He set them on their feet, and told them to sit quietly near their mother. "Be careful of her," he warned. "She is very precious. And we must look after her."

Catherine smiled up into his eyes. Never had she loved him so much as at this moment.

"Your Majesty, there is someone to see you." One of her courtiers bowed before her, his face grave.

Suddenly her mouth was dry. "Is it bad news?"

"Your Majesty, a messenger has come from France. The Duke of Bedford is dead."

Catherine felt the room spin around her. John, good kind John, protector of her son's interest, was dead. She felt tears slide down her cheeks, and she was not ashamed of them.

"There must be a special Mass," she whispered. "That is all we can do for him now."

Suddenly the day seemed dark. There were no good omens after all; only the news of death. She sent her ladies away and sat on the bed holding her shawl around her body for comfort.

Owen knelt before her. "Come, Catherine, this is the way of life; there is a death and there will be a birth. We cannot alter the shape of things."

She clung to him. "John was a good man. He loved Henry, and cared devotedly for him. The others will just use my son to get power for themselves."

"Don't distress yourself, Catherine; we will guard him. He will come to no harm. Just think, in only a few years, he will be out of tutelage, and then no one will be able to dictate to him."

Catherine shook her head. "You know how weak he is."

Owen kissed her. "I love you dearly, Catherine. I will protect you and the children. Don't you worry about that." Catherine rubbed her head against his shoulder. "Yes, darling one, I know you will."

She closed her eyes for a moment, wondering who would protect him if she was not there.

–

Catherine looked with curiosity, as the coach stopped, and a young good-looking man alighted. After him came a girl who seemed vaguely familar. Catherine smiled; she was carrying a child in her arms. The couple were stopped and then moved forward again. She felt Owen stiffen beside her, and then she realised that the girl was Lady Margaret.

"Come inside, Catherine," Owen said quickly. "I don't want you to be upset any more today." She glanced up at him and saw that his face was flushed.

"Why should I be upset, my lord?" she said, resisting his hand as he tried to draw her away.

Lady Margaret was dipping awkwardly before her, and at her side, the elegant Lord Kilbourn bowed respectfully.

Catherine watched as Margaret looked at Owen, her yellow eyes flashing some sort of message. What could it be? Surely the girl was married now, and very well married by the expensive look about her.

"This is no time to ask for an audience with the Queen," Owen said sharply. "She has had bad news from France today, and she should be resting."

At once Margaret made to move away, but Lord Kilbourn turned and caught her arm.

"We do not wish to distress Your Majesty; perhaps you could spare us some time, my lord?"

Catherine looked from one to the other, and imperiously ordered them to come inside the chamber.

"I will know what this is all about," she said firmly. "If there is one thing I can't stand, it is a mystery."

She was breathless by the time she reached her chamber. She sat carefully in the cushioned chair, glad to relax. The sun had made her eyes ache, and she felt faintly dizzy.

"Be seated," she said.

Lady Margaret was standing awkwardly, like a young colt, her eyes full of pain and her slim shoulders slumped. Owen, too, looked careworn; in fact it was only Lord Kilbourn who seemed to have a smile on his face.

"Now what is this all about? Do you need help in any way?"

Silence greeted her words and then softly, Margaret began to cry. The baby in her arms stirred, and whimpered; and she hugged it close, her tears falling faster than ever. Lord Kilbourn had a sardonic smile on his face that was quickly beginning to irritate. He moved over to the child and drew back the covering so that the red silky hair was exposed. Margaret did not look up. She merely sobbed into the silence of the room.

Suddenly everything was clear to Catherine. "What is it you want, Lord Kilbourn? Money I suppose?"

"Your Majesty, I have only good intentions. I felt it just…"

Catherine held up her hand for silence and she seemed to grow in stature.

"Guards!" she said, and immediately the doors opened and her men awaited her command. "This man has laid his hands on a royal personage; it is treason. Remove him to a place of imprisonment."

She stared at him stonily, as he pleaded with her to release him.

"I will consider what is to be done with you at some later date," she said remorselessly. "Your wife may return to her home and keep her possessions;

all of them," she said pointedly. "Now leave me. Everyone. I wish to be alone."

She stood in silence long after they had left, and the sound of their footsteps had died away. Several times, Owen tried to approach her, but she didn't want to see him; she didn't want to see anybody.

She curled herself up on the bed, not even allowing Marie near her. What was the use of anything? What was living for? She thought back to when her first daughter had died. It was then that Owen took Margaret, and she, Catherine had forgiven him for it. But she hadn't known then that there was to be a child. How could she bring herself to forgive and forget such a thing as that?

The night dropped down, and Catherine still lay alone in her chamber. She wanted no tapers lit; she wanted to curl up and stay like a little winter animal, separated from the world and from reality. The day that had begun with so much promise was ending, and the results of it were pain and heartbreak. John of Bedford was dead and now her heart was dead because of Owen's faithlessness.

Chapter Nineteen

"So John is dead. God rest his soul. He was a fine honest man."

Humphrey sat up in his bed, the ache in his chest having eased a little; even his cautious physicians had said he was a little better. They stood around him now, eyes watchful for any adverse signs.

"He was a good brother, and I shall see to it that his work in France continues as he would have wished."

He looked down at the documents in his hand. Phillip of Burgundy was calling for a conference between his own people, and the English and French, and he, Humphrey, Regent of England, would go personally to Arras to see that the Burgundian Duke did not play any tricks.

"Bring my clothes!" he commanded, disregarding the consternation his words caused. "I must be up and about again."

He felt good as his feet touched the floor. He was fit for many years yet, and perhaps he would obey his advisers and forgo the rich food and wine that he loved so much.

He smiled smugly. That fool, the Cardinal, had thought him already in his grave. He had seen the calculating look in the old man's eyes, as he watched him writhe on the floor in agony; but he would see that Humphrey was not so easily disposed of.

He whistled merrily as he walked along the corridors. France and Phillip of Burgundy would toe the line once he showed them he was no weakling, and would not be trifled with; but in the meantime, he might as well find his amusements where he could.

–

"Mother, please let me speak to you."

Catherine looked languidly at her eldest son, as he bent over her. His face was pinched and white, and she wondered impatiently what was wrong with him now.

"Yes, come sit beside my bed, Henry. Surely those are not tears I see in your eyes? And you a big lad of thirteen?" Her voice was soft, in spite of her irritation, and she folded his hand between hers, drawing him nearer.

"May I stay here with you and Owen, mother? The children are very fond of me, and I of them." He fidgeted a little as he attempted to explain. "Since my Uncle Humphrey became Regent, I don't really know what is expected of me. I am torn in opposite directions because the Cardinal advises me differently to my uncle."

Catherine sighed. "Neither of them are speaking in your interest, my son; you must listen to them both, and try to form your own opinion."

Henry looked dejected. "It is so difficult, mother, but I'll try." His face brightened. "When Edmund and Jasper grow up, they will help me, won't they? I know they love me."

"Yes, they do love you, Henry," Catherine smiled fondly. "I hope you will remember that, and allow no one to turn you against them. Remember, they are your half-brothers, and deserve respect from others."

"I will always look after them, Mother. I promise you."

She kissed his cheek. "You are a good boy, Henry; too good perhaps for the position you hold. You are so trusting."

"But I may stay here, mother, is that not so?" He looked so anxious that Catherine hugged him impulsively.

"You may stay for a while, until Humphrey of Gloucester decides which form of tuition you will receive next. In any case, he is to go to France; so I do not think he will be concerned with you for the present." She patted his cheek. "Now go and play; enjoy the sunshine and your freedom, and let me get some rest."

She lay back wearily. Why couldn't Henry have been strong like his father? It would be so good to know that her future and the future of her other children would be in strong hands.

"Catherine, are you sleeping?"

She turned her head slowly to look at Owen. His face was drawn, and anxious. She held her hand out to him; and thankfully, he took it.

"Yesterday," she said quietly, "I think I almost hated you. But today, I am of a softer frame of mind; and in any event, nothing seems to matter a great deal."

"How are you feeling, Catherine? Are there any pains yet?" Owen sat carefully beside her, his hands still holding hers.

She shook her head. "I feel nothing except utter weariness. Sit beside me and I will try to sleep."

She closed her eyes, and the dark lashes sank like shadows against the pale skin of her cheeks. The fresh flush of health seemed to have left her once more, and she was a small, defenceless woman in an enormous bed.

–

Catherine thought she was in a dream, and her body was being encircled by skirts grown too tight for her. Then she opened her eyes, and realised that her labour had begun. Marie was walking softly, preparing already for the birth.

"How did you know before I did?" Catherine asked in amazement.

Marie smiled. "I always know, my lady. I know everything about you. I should do. I've served you long enough." She brought a cup to Catherine. "Drink this, it will help; though I don't think this labour is going to take long. Your daughter will be born before the sun rises."

Catherine felt her spirits rise. God be praised if Marie was right. She was so tired that she could not spend hours struggling to bring her child into the world. She felt she would die in the attempt.

"Does Owen know?" she said softly, and Marie nodded continuing with her preparations. "He will be glad when it is all over," Catherine said, wincing as the pain began again. "He says there must be no more children for me after this; he wants me to be well and strong."

Marie moved around the bed. "Hush, my lady; the physicians will be here soon. I don't want them to think I have allowed you to tire yourself. Try to go with the pain. Let it carry you along. You must not fight it."

Catherine smiled. "You are right, Marie, you are always right! I am in your excellent hands."

—

Jacina was born just before sunrise, a healthy, lovely baby girl. Her hair was red like her father's, but her eyes were dark, almost black.

"Just look, my lady! She is beautiful; oh! a lovely child. Are you not delighted, my lady?"

Marie was beside herself with joy, and Catherine smiled with tears in her eyes.

"Owen, what do you think of her? Oh, God be praised for giving me so much joy."

Catherine's face was radiant, and as Owen knelt beside her, his heart quickened with hope. Perhaps now, they could begin afresh. He would make sure that nothing he did would ever upset the Queen again.

"She is the most beautiful child I've ever seen." He held the tiny dimpled fingers and stared in wonder at the perfectly formed nails. "Our daughter; she is almost as beautiful as her mother."

"Her Majesty must rest now," Marie said, and immediately took charge of the sickroom, ushering everyone, including Owen, outside. "She must sleep, so that she can regain her strength."

Catherine lay back, grateful for the silence. It was wonderful to have the birth over, and to know that the daughter she had longed for was strong and healthy.

"I am so happy, Marie," she murmured, her eyes drooping with tiredness. "I will rest, and then when I feel better, we will celebrate; but I will think of that later."

She closed her eyes and relaxed, dimly conscious of Marie's hands drawing the covers closer over her shoulders. It was good to be cared for in this way.

–

Marie sat by the bed, watching the Queen. Her cheeks seemed shrunken, and her eyes had become even more deep-set. There was an unhealthy tinge of yellow under the skin, and Catherine seemed to have aged greatly in the two weeks since her child had been born.

"My head aches, Marie." Catherine pulled herself up against the pillows with difficulty, and her dark eyes glittered as if with fever.

Marie rose at once, anxious to make Catherine more comfortable. She shook the pillow, and held a cup to the Queen's lips.

"Here, my lady; some wine will do you good. And perhaps now you could bring yourself to eat something?"

Gasping a little, Catherine shook her head. "Not just now. My bones ache, and somehow even the feel of the air against my flesh gives me pain." She lay back exhausted, and closed her eyes. "It is taking me a long time to recover from the birth of my little

Jacina. But she is worth all the discomfort. Bring her to me Marie, please."

Reluctantly, Marie brought the baby to the Queen's bedside. It seemed that Catherine's arms had become too frail to hold even such a tiny child.

"Just look at the way her hair curls. She is going to break some hearts when she grows up."

A fond smile lightened Catherine's face, so that for a moment she seemed almost her former self; and Marie's spirits lifted. Perhaps, given time, Catherine would be well again, issuing orders in her charming but imperious way.

Marie had become more devout lately. Perhaps by following the Queen's example. Every night she prayed that her lady would regain her health. It was heartbreaking to see the Queen so tired and weak.

"See how she stares at me." Catherine kissed the tiny face of her daughter, holding her close. "I feel I won't be spared to enjoy my baby for very long."

Marie turned sharply, a sick feeling gripping her stomach. "Oh, my lady! Don't say such a thing."

She stood looking in dismay at the Queen, as tears ran fast and bitter down her thin cheeks, as she cradled the child.

"You have been ill before." Marie forced herself to speak naturally. "Remember how ill you were when little Margaret was taken away from us? Yet you recovered from that despair, and lived to be strong. Now you have everything in the world you could wish for."

Catherine shook her head. "I have this premonition, Marie, and much as I might wish to live, to be with my husband and children, I feel it will not be." She bent her head and did not meet Marie's eyes. "I am tired, so terribly weary, that dying would almost come as a relief."

Marie gulped hard and went to Catherine's side. "Oh, my lady," she said brokenly.

Catherine looked at her with a touch of animation in her gaunt face. "I don't wish Owen to hear any of this. Allow him to believe that I am slowly improving. I could not bear to see his distress." She paused a moment, to collect her thoughts. "In spite of everything, I know that Owen has truly loved me in all our years together. He has been a wonderful husband, and I do not regret any of it; so don't cry for me." She lay back a moment to recover her breath. "Now bring me fresh clothes and help me to sit beside the bed. Let them all see the Queen is out of her childbed, and is not dead yet."

The pain inside Marie was almost impossible to bear, as she did as Catherine requested. She was closer to the Queen than anyone, except her husband, and she knew that the Queen spoke the truth! Catherine was slowly dying.

–

"Ah, so Phillip has deserted the English. I thought it would not take him long."

Catherine sat near the window with her back to the sunshine; her long hair was combed forward in a new style that softened the sharpened contours of her face. She had dressed most carefully, and no one would suspect that each time she moved, her thin limbs ached intolerably.

"It is a good thing John has not lived to see this." Owen crouched on the floor at the Queen's feet. "He spent his lifetime working to keep Paris and the throne for young Henry."

"Yes, but now Humphrey insists that the defeats have come about through mismanagement," Catherine said quietly. "He cannot see how well Charles has built up the army, and the country's resources. In fact, I am surprised at my brother's success myself. I admit it."

She shifted her position carefully but Owen was quick to notice.

"Another cushion, Catherine?" He jumped up and tried to make her more comfortable.

Catherine laughed, and held up her hand. "Owen, can't I even breathe without you worrying over me?" She touched his hand gently. "I know your concern, but I wish you would stop worrying. I am all right; can't you see that I am feeling better today?"

He smiled. She did look better, though her hand trembled in his and her lips were too pale.

"I wonder how Charles feels about me," Catherine said a little wistfully. "It would be wonderful if we could take our family to France for a time."

Owen grunted sceptically. "I can't see the King of France holding out a hand to welcome the young King of England; even if he is his nephew. Perhaps, without the interference of Humphrey and the Bishop, such a thing would have been possible, but at this present time such a move would be folly."

He stared at Catherine indulgently. "Don't tell me you are homesick, after all these years?"

Catherine gazed out through the window. "I would have liked to see France once more," she said thoughtfully; then she smiled. "Soon I will be too old to travel." Her voice was deliberately light. "I am almost thirty-six years of age, and the mother of six children." She crossed herself. "God rest the soul of little Margaret."

Owen frowned. "What is it, Catherine? Does something ail you, that you haven't told me about?" He took her face in his hands and suddenly read the truth in her eyes. She closed them quickly; but it was too late. He dropped to his knees, and wrapped his arms around her waist. "Don't leave me, Catherine. I cannot live without you." He put his face into her lap, and her hands were soft on his hair.

"We must both be strong, Owen," she said, her voice thick with tears. "I would rather have kept it from you, but you are too sensitive to my feelings." She took a deep breath. "Try not to grieve; we have a little time left. We must make all our remaining days happy ones."

She drew his face up to hers, and their lips met in a mingling of pain and love. And to Owen, it seemed that Catherine had already said goodbye to him.

Chapter Twenty

The flowers growing in the hedgerows lifted bright faces to the hot sun, and their perfume drifting across the scented June air, brought a contentment to Catherine, so that the journey seemed less arduous.

"Isn't it a lovely day, boys?" she smiled at her sons; and Edmund thoughtful as ever answered her politely.

"I'd like to play outside, Mother; perhaps go down to the stream to watch the fish. Will we go there again soon?"

Catherine smiled sadly. "I expect you will play there a great deal Edmund. And catch many fish. But just now we are going to visit a friend of mine." She tapped Jasper gently as he pulled at his brother's coat. "Be good now, or your father will be cross!"

The coach rumbled on, and Owen, with Jacina in his arms, had fallen asleep. Catherine smiled softly. No wonder he was tired. He had spent most of the night trying to coax some life back into her numb limbs. He never lost patience, or gave up hope; that in spite of everything, she would recover.

She looked out at the green grass and the tall trees reaching leafy fingers to the sky, and knew that she would not see another summer.

"Mother, I want to ride on the horse!" Jasper jumped excitedly from his seat, his sturdy young body, quick and eager.

Catherine caught him close, and kissed his red hair, "Calm down, my son; you must be patient. The journey is nearly over."

As she spoke, the grey walls of Bermondsey Abbey appeared on the horizon, and mingled with her relief that soon she would be with the good Abbess and her sisters, was regret that from now on the gay, colourful world of the court would be lost to her forever.

"Owen, we are there." She had hardly spoken the words than he was awake, his strong hands reaching out to cover her own.

"You will be in good hands here; and perhaps your friend, the Abbess, will be able to help you more than I have done." He tried to smile and Catherine was unable to kill his hopes altogether.

"Yes, she is very experienced at caring for those who are sick. But I cannot see that anyone on this earth could do more for me than you have done."

Jasper leaned out to look at the abbey. His blue eyes filled with excitement, because he was in a new place. Soon he would know every corner of the mellow building; his sharp eyes would seek out all its secrets. He had a mind like a magpie. He hoarded images and sensations. Above him, he saw the sky blotted out for a moment as the carriage passed under the gateway, and then it was all excitement as the lady in a long dark gown, that rubbed roughly against his cheek, lifted him down to the ground.

—

Marie closed the last lock of the chest with a snap. Now everything of Catherine's was packed away; her trinkets, the red dress she'd loved so much – there they were all hidden from sight. It was strange, almost eerie, as if the Queen was already dead.

Marie shuddered. This was the first time in her life that she'd been parted from Catherine, and she felt as if a part of herself was missing. Something that even the presence of her husband and child couldn't make up for.

"You may go now." One of the ladies of the court stood at the chamber door. To her Marie was nothing but a servant, who had risen above her station by the indulgence of the Queen.

Marie put her hands on her hips. "Yes, I will go now; what is there left to keep me?"

She strode past the gaping woman and left the royal apartments. Soon, she and Tom, and their son, would move to the house near the abbey, the house that the Queen had bought for them, at the same time as she had settled a pension on Marie.

"I want you to be independent," she'd said smiling in her old vivacious way, "so that you can keep an eye on my family for me."

There were tears in Marie's eyes as she thought about it. She loved Catherine, as if she was indeed related by blood as the gossips had said, and she understood the Queen's desire to see her settled with no need to beg from anyone.

She left quietly without looking back. She had always changed homes when the Queen did, and this time was going to be no different.

The sun blazed down and for a moment, Marie saw nothing but the orange glare in the bright sky; then she heard voices, sharp and clear on the still air.

"Why has the Queen left her residence? I have come from France to see her."

Holding her hand to shield her eyes, Marie saw Humphrey of Gloucester seated on his horse, a large shape against the sky.

The murmured reply from the Queen's secretary was lost on Marie, but she saw Humphrey stiffen in the saddle.

"My God! I hadn't realised she was as bad as that."

There was a note of triumph in his voice that set Marie's teeth on edge. If she had a blade about her she would have thrown it straight for his heart; and damn the consequences.

"Well, in that case, I need detain you no longer." Humphrey wheeled his horse around. "His Majesty must be brought to his mother's bedside. Where has the Queen been taken?"

The unsuspecting secretary gave the information readily, and Humphrey chuckled.

"Now we shall see how great a man is this Owen Tudor. No longer will he hide behind his wife's skirts."

The sound of the galloping horse beat into Marie's head. She would have to warn Owen that Humphrey would take his revenge if he could.

–

The walls of the abbey were deep and cool, and Catherine was grateful for the comfort she found there. The Abbess was a serene woman, and an honest one. She made no attempt to conceal the fact that she knew Catherine was dying. Calmly she went about her duties, her hands gentle and practical, as if they tended royalty every day of the year.

"You will care for my children?" Catherine could scarcely bring the words out for the tears that choked her. "I know that while in these walls, they will be safe from anyone who seeks to harm them."

The Abbess inclined her head. "They will be safe, have no fear on that account." She helped Catherine to sit up against the pillows. "Look outside; the children play very happily under the trees."

Jasper was shouting and pulling at Edmund's arm until he agreed to climb up into the sturdy branches.

"The summer has gone by so quickly," Catherine said. "The leaves are almost the same colour as my children's hair." She smiled at the Abbess. "My months here have been peaceful ones. I wonder how many more such I will have."

The Abbess smiled. "Only God knows the answer to that, Your Majesty."

Catherine watched the boys for a few moments longer, and then her strength deserted her, and she slipped back, her face almost white as the sheets.

"Where is my husband?" she asked breathlessly. "He seems to have been away from me for some time."

She worried constantly about him. Several times she had begged him to return to the mountains of his home country where he would be safe from Humphrey's anger. But he would not leave her, and she felt warm inside when she thought of him.

"I believe he went to visit his friends. He is to bring Marie with him, to see you today."

Catherine nodded. "Yes, I remember now; he told me. I hope he will not be long."

She turned her face to the wall, shutting out the brightness of the autumn sun. She had so little time, and she wanted her loved ones with her every moment.

–

"She is weaker, but at peace with herself."

Owen sat on the wooden chair, his arms folded before him. At his side sat Marie, her face filled with pain and compassion.

"I wish there was more I could do. I have always been with my lady, to tend to her and care for her from the time we were both children."

From outside came the sound of horses, and quickly Marie ran to the door, her heart beating fast. Owen sat stiff in his chair, his hand fingering the knife in his belt.

"It is Tom." Marie was weak with relief. "He has brought another pair of horses. For a moment I thought…"

"I don't mind too much what Humphrey does," Owen said, "but if he tried to take me away from Catherine while she is still alive, I would go mad." He drank from the cup Marie put before him. "I don't think he would dare attempt anything just yet; he will hold his hand until… later."

Marie nodded in agreement. "Yes, I feel that; but even so, be very wary, my lord. I trust him as I trust a viper."

Tom came and sat near the crackling fire. "Sorry if I startled you; I didn't think." He rubbed his hands. "The air grows crisp. I'm glad of a fire, Marie." Watching him, Owen marvelled at how little Thomas Cooper had changed in the twenty or so years he had known him. He was still as strong and agile as the day they set sail for Agincourt. That was a lifetime ago! The only reminder of it all was Tom's stiff arm and the awkward way he sometimes held his head when the old wound in his neck seemed to be giving him trouble.

Now, he sat here in his snug little house with Marie, and a strong fine son sleeping in his bed. A lucky man indeed! But then none of them had thought in those far-off days that one day Owen Tudor would marry Catherine of France, widow of the King. In spite of the sadness that was always with him now, Owen knew he wouldn't change his life one bit from its course.

"I'd better be getting back to the Abbey."

He rose almost reluctantly, much as he wanted to be with Catherine; the pain of it all was sometimes unbearable.

"I will be ready in a moment." Marie wrapped herself warmly for the ride, and kissed Tom's cheek. She clung to him for a moment. "I will be back before dark," she said, her eyes filling with tears.

He put his hand out to her. "Take your time, my love; the Queen needs you more than I do at this time."

Together, Marie and Owen left the house and rode across the fields that were sharp with the smell of rotting leaves. Soon the branches would be bare, and winter would be laying cold hands on the country.

–

"The King is here to see you, Your Majesty."

Vaguely, Catherine saw the slim figure of Henry, her son, standing at the bedside. She tried to smile, and beckoned that he should sit near to her.

"How old are you now, Henry?" she whispered, praying that he had become more of a man since she'd last seen him.

"I'm fourteen, Mother." His voice was soft, with a hint of tears in it. "How are you feeling today? A little better, I pray."

She inclined her head. "Henry, promise me that you will care for your brothers, and for little Jacina." She stopped, fighting for breath. "Remember they are descended from the same womb as you are; and they deserve royal favour."

Henry nodded firmly. "As God is my judge, Mother, I will care for them. I love them, you see."

He closed his mouth in the stubborn way that weak people often have, and Catherine felt a great sense of joy grow inside her. There was no doubt that no one would change Henry's mind on that matter, at least.

"I don't know what you can do for Owen Tudor, my son; but he has been a true father to you in everything but fact. If you can shield him, my son, do so."

It was difficult for her to go on, and alarmed, Henry called out for someone to come.

Catherine shook her head. "I am all right," she protested. "I feel a little weak, that is all."

Owen sat beside her and gathered her frail form into his arms. "Please, Catherine, don't try to speak.

You will wear yourself out." Gently he pushed back her hair from her forehead beaded with sweat and pulled the covers over her shoulders.

Catherine fixed dark eyes once more on her son. "Remember, Henry, what you have promised."

He bowed his head to hide his tears and twisted his white slender hands together. "I will remember, Mother. Please do not distress yourself." He stepped away from the bed realising that no one could dismiss the King. "I will leave you now, Mother. I will take Edmund and Jasper outside for a while."

Catherine watched him go, a look of peace on her thin face. Her hand groped for Owen's and they clung together knowing that this would be the final goodbye.

"Go to Wales, I beg of you, my love, so that you will be safe. I will be with you every step of the way in spirit, you know that."

Unable to speak Owen nodded, and desperately tried to summon a smile. Catherine lifted her hand to touch his red hair, that sprung bright as ever over his brow, then her eyes became misty, and her hand dropped like a discarded petal on to the bedcover.

—

Outside the abbey, the snow was deep and the pale January sun shone on the red hair of Edmund Tudor. The bells began to toll, but the young boy had no idea of the meaning behind the mournful sound.

"When I am a man, I shall have a son; and he will be Henry, after you," he said, trying to comfort his half-brother, who although he was King of England, unaccountably had tears in his eyes.

But Henry didn't hear. He looked away over the small boy's head, unaware that the Tudor tree had begun to blossom.